TO DAYS OF YORE

by

Lillie Lane

A GOSHEN PUBLISHERS BOOK VIRGINIA

TO DAYS OF YORE

ISBN: 978-1959702214

Copyright ©2023 Lillie Lane

Library of Congress Cataloging-in-Publication Data

Published in 2023 by:

GOSHEN PUBLISHERS LLC
P.O. Box 1562
Stephens City, Virginia, USA

www.GoshenPublishers.com

Our books may be purchased in bulk for promotional, educational, or business use. For inquiries, please contact the publisher via email: Agents@GoshenPublishers.com.

First Edition 2023

Cover designed by Goshen Publishers LLC

Dedication

To Elias, thank you for hugging my neck and teaching me how to make the best of life. To Kent, Kael, and Karlo, thank you for inspiring me and teaching me in more ways than you could ever know. To my parents, thank you for pushing me to read early and often. I haven't stopped since. To my family, thank you for your unwavering support and for your stories and laughs. All of it went into this book. To Ms. Ross, thank you for believing in my writing and equipping me with the black book. That is one of my most cherished keepsakes.

"Never forget the bridge that carries you over."
– E.R. Dinsmoor

Thank you tremendously to those who helped me get across and to those who paved the way.

Contents

Dedication, iii

Introduction, 1

Chapter One, 5

Chapter Two, 10

Chapter Three, 17

Chapter Four, 27

Chapter Five, 37

Chapter Six, 47

Chapter Seven, 58

Chapter Eight, 66

Chapter Nine, 77

Chapter Ten, 83

Chapter Eleven, 90

Chapter Twelve, 97

Chapter Thirteen, 103

Chapter Fourteen, 116

Chapter Fifteen, 126

Chapter Sixteen , 138

Chapter Seventeen, 149

Chapter Eighteen, 155

Introduction

I know no one does this anymore...but therein lies my intent. I've been dreaming of moments like this back since I can remember. No one around me shared my burning desire to toil away at a desk for hours writing a novel. It was early in the 21st century, and we were accelerating towards the technology era—one with shorter attention spans and seemingly less adoration for books in general. Before now, it was hard to imagine a world that was so connected you didn't need to get lost in fiction to take your body and mind elsewhere; one that no longer knew the nostalgic smells of fresh pencil shavings commingled with the sounds of mounted sharpeners squeaking over the voices of grade-school teachers. Far removed from those days are modern times and technology.

Yet I sat down one day to write this story. And eleven years later, I emerged, back-broken and arthritic from sitting hunched over with an ever-so-slightly bent wrist, ignoring the pains of carpal tunnel to emancipate the emotions churning inside of me. I had to tell this story.

If you know me, you understand that once I set my mind to something, I'm determined to do it—even if it means sacrificing the unthinkable. Pressure makes diamonds, and I'm insistent on earning everything the hard way.

Early in my life I made a theme of taking the harder route to each of my various destinations, and because this work serves as a representation of my life, I see it fitting that I maintain a level of consistency and accuracy for the record. Hard truths can sometimes heal those soft spots. Perhaps it is those tedious and toilsome journeys that incite our belief in a greater power as imperative to our subsistence. In my quest

Lillie Lane

for healing, I discovered my love of naturopathic medicine, and from the riches of the Earth, I found God.

In a world that has discounted the contributions of Black Americans to every sector of society and diminished our place in the central fabric of our nation's history, the stories and traditions that have been passed down through generations are the oft forgotten pieces of a puzzle that connects our past to the present day. From our food to our religion and everything in between, the origins of the information conveyed by our forefathers has sometimes been lost in oral translation. From incidental misinterpretations to intentional misrepresentations made by those with ill intentions, some of us have been led to believe the blasphemy that has blemished the legends of Afro-American legacies. Many have referred to our ancestral practices as dark, demonic, and unsophisticated, disregarding our influence on the arts and medicine and other STEAM disciplines. This book is, in part, an attempt to shift that inaccurate narrative.

For the record:

I'm KC. I was born in a big city on the East Coast bustling with lights, sounds, and the desperate dreams of a population tormented by its ancestral past. It was that predominantly Black suburb reeking with the political redolence of the Capitol's failed agendas that formulated my ideas of rebellion and created an iron will against injustice in every aspect. Those hard streets formed a raging insurgent against the constraints of authority and society's classist limitations. They birthed a king destined to claim his rightful throne, his destiny. And so it was...the makings of a masterpiece.

You see, with greatness comes great expectations, grandiose demands from the lips of all who bear witness to your talents...anticipating the day you unlock your potential and fulfill your purpose to Planet Earth. The road to greatness—as nearly every young aspirant shall find—is long, rough, and rugged. It takes grit, it takes resilience, it takes the heart of a champion to rise up and seize what lies atop the heights of life. This is the story of that ascent, and of those along for the journey. Heavy was the load and treacherous was the path we took, learning lessons with every fiery step towards fate. Here's to those burning sands and days of yore…

Release Your Inhibitions

I walk in...she looks at me, I look at her,
I begin to lick my lips. My heart starts pounding, my
 senses begin to tingle,
I am hot; emotions take over as she just sits there and
 stares into my soul,
teasing me, seducing me with her sultry swagger as she
 dances across the pages of my mind,
all of me in thrall to the allure of her audacious
 composition…
Now bound by these words and these very pages to
 which I profess myself to her—
This is literature. This is love.

Chapter One

I flinched at the loud clang of the steel door behind me after what seemed the millionth time. Despite nearly a decade of confinement, the sound of metal locking me even tighter into this decrepit dungeon remained unnerving. Feeling "secure" in a maximum-security prison was to admit defeat and acquiesce to the atrocities of life behind bars.

I was consumed with anxiety over my release date and stumbling my way through the last two weeks of a ten-year stint in a human zoo. I'd taken the time to hone one of my most cherished crafts, becoming one hell of a jailhouse writer. As a young boy, I'd loved to climb to the highest point of a tree I could reach, prop my feet up on a limb, and sit for hours writing about the world from a bird's-eye view. Little did I know that one day the places I'd go would offer much better views of life's most precious moments from which to draw upon for my work. I leaned into literature to fuel my purpose and I aimed to plant money trees with the seeds of wisdom embedded in my words. If life was a movie, mine was made for primetime. A journey isn't complete without a dozen or more janky experiences along the way to share with your friends and find blessings in or learn lessons from. It's just too bad those stories don't pay as well as they tell.

It's true what they say about money being the root of all evil. The desperation that derives from destitution has dictated the fates of countless young men who fall victim to their love of money. The power possessed in currency is undeniable for sure. I could tell you every story of my life and most of them have a connection to money—either the gift of having it or the lack thereof. The dilutive effect of dollars drove me nearly to destruction, but it also led me to a remarkable revelation.

Following the money trail opened my eyes to the reality of the matrix. Capitalism kept the rat race going, and power hoarders paid substantial sums to ensure the masses remained in a perpetual state of oblivion upheld by a fabulous façade. The world around us is fraught with falsity posing as truth. We consume it subconsciously, creating a conscious conformity to the will of the wicked that hampers the manumission of men from their monetary masters.

I remember back before I even understood the concept of having capital, living comfortably in what would be considered poverty by today's standards. Hell, more often than not, we had more hopes and dreams than we did money in our pockets. We were programmed to remain bloodthirsty and steadfast in that race toward the ultimate reward, chasing after the one thing that seemed to give us all life. In the years, months, and days I've sat in this jail cell, though, I've had plenty of time to ponder the forgotten promises that befall the formerly chosen as they become the cast-aside. Most guys in here spend their time plotting; scheming for a way out or reading classic literature and law books to "enlighten" themselves or lifting weights. Me? I do the same thing every day. I sit there on my bed surrounded by those four cold walls, and I ponder on this constant principle. I think about money; day in, day out, whether alone or on the yard for PT.

Every thought that could be induced by green dollar signs has crossed my mind once or twice throughout my tenure here. The introduction of fiat currency into society accelerated the fateful end of many sustaining empires, people, and principles. Whoever the bastard was that came up with that ingenious idea to make currency the means of power was the smartest, cruelest asshole ever formed by God's hands. Some might even say, insofar as the world is concerned, he IS God. The key to a prosperous life, no matter what you say or hear, is money.

Money drove me to lengths I never thought I would take to acquire it. Death was never a fear of mine. Being poor was. Living in poverty is the equivalent of being invisible in many ways. I couldn't bear to live life in the shadows and so I developed an insatiable hunger for mastering the art of the hustle. Of course, every hustle wasn't always legit. I wasn't your average outlaw though. Every community has their Robin Hood, and I was all about taking old money to make it new. Economic wealth redistribution has been an illusive concept under our system of capitalism for most of society's existence. Leveraging "dirty" dollars earned at the expense of the poor to counter corporate and criminal exploitation was principle to my business.

While those practices were always well-intentioned, they didn't always come out clean. Sometimes I walked away with blood on my hands. The power of money has an influence that turns the straightest of men crooked. It'll fulfill your every desire or set your life and your dreams ablaze in a quarry of fire. The ultimate foundation to a world of pain, hurt, and destruction is to place in it a symbol or object that will forever pit people against each other. A sick, twisted mind is the only thing capable of creating a plan so cruel, so unnatural, that it would be a cause for eternal conflict amongst humans. I dismissed the carnage created consequent to my conquests as a necessary sacrifice in order to accomplish the mission of liberation.

As I grew up, I began to suffer more and more from the pains of ambition. When you shoot for the stars, landing amongst the clouds just doesn't seem quite good enough.

My ideas of changing the world, making an impact, building bridges, and being good to others compelled a need to be rich enough to afford the joys of philanthropy and influence. I used to think that the key to happiness, power, and your heart's utmost desires lies in the hands of the almighty dollar. Either you have it, or you don't, and the most blood-curdling and wicked acts are done out of the desire for a piece of it. I lost myself in that pursuit. Autonomy and achievement became an excuse to be on the constant attack. Yet who was I liberating if not myself? How could I preach freedom when I had become captive to my own self-destruction? Of course, it wasn't always like this...

Makings of a Masterpiece

Ma chère, how exquisite our embrace,
The paroxysm of unbridled purpose absorbing the pain
    of broken picture frames,
The fever of forgotten elements igniting infernos of
    imagination within,
Limbs offer labor that gives way to lethargy;
We languish in the lust of our ambitions,
Toiling away until dreams become destiny,
Making up for the lives lost to chagrin,
Sweeping sweat from the furrowed brows of weary but
    winsome men,
Reclaiming peace through the power of the pen,
Inhale, exhale, release…
These moments are the makings of a masterpiece.

Lillie Lane

Chapter Two

I glanced around at the other glazed faces of students who were struggling to keep up at this point in the lecture. Long days took a toll towards the end of the week. We went to school from eight in the morning to five in the evening every day, and once each month on Saturday. It was fucking brutal. Our "no excuses" model and unconventional schedule was supposed to be in preparation for the rigors of life beyond adolescence; a college preparatory school, they called it.

The tensions that still existed across color lines in southern society and its school systems offered a daily dose of irony. Here I was, roaming the halls of a school named after President Lincoln on the same false premise that made him celebrated as the man whose moral compass compelled him to end slavery. Lincoln High's mission purported to free young Black minds from prison pipelines and propel them towards the promise of a better life, but there was an element of truth missing. It wasn't really the school's primary objective to see us succeed; that was simply collateral to the profits realized as a result of government-funded experiential grants. Our ancestors were fighters, and our blood was filled with the same passion that sent slaves rising up against their oppressors. Lincoln's resources helped us maximize our capacities for changing the world through our own agendas. The abuse we endured along the way fueled the fires that we would eventually set to the world.

A book thudded to the floor as I was dozing off again. I pulled out my phone to check the time and send a quick message to my brother telling him to meet me behind the school when it let out. I feigned interest in the crude illustrations of quadratic equations applied to bridge suspensions and business revenue calculations that were scribbled across the board.

5, 4, 3, 2, 1... "Rinnnnng!!" The bell pierced through classrooms and hallways, cutting conversations short and sending a surge of excitement in the air with its call. Mr. Maxton shouted a few more words about next week's homework that were muffled as the door flew open and excited voices drowned him out. I threw my books in my bag and ran out the door before he could try to signal my attention. I scurried past my locker, past the crowds of students emptying their lockers for the weekend because I didn't need any books. All of my work was done on Monday mornings before school. It was a routine that had worked for me since middle school, and my procrastination had spoiled me into thinking that this was a solid plan for academic success. As I rushed out the doors of the school, I saw a crowd of students approaching from the neighboring high school. One of them that I didn't recognize called out to me and caught me by surprise. I was pretty lowkey, so for anyone outside of my immediate networks to know me was rare. Hearing my nickname was even more of a shocker, because I'd always thought of it as a relatively intimate moniker amongst small circles.

My name is Kameron Cole, but you can call me KC. I look nothing like my namesake from the collab group with Jojo, but I've heard those jokes pretty much all my life. I'm an introvert—an ISTP according to Meyers-Briggs. Because of that, my relationships with others are often strained by a constant need for personal space and time to myself, all alone with just my thoughts. I was born with an air of mystery that frequently leaves people trying to place their finger on me, albeit inaccurately. My deep distrust of people developed naturally as I grew up in stifling surroundings, and I often offered miscues as a safety mechanism when presenting my persona. I believe humans are multi-faceted individuals who weren't meant to be placed into particular boxes, but who could place themselves in them by acting accordingly and consistently. A famed philosopher once said strikingly, "We are what we repeatedly do. Excellence then is not an act, but a habit."

That quote stuck with me on the back of my class t-shirt my final year of high school and through adulthood. I later ended up getting a tattoo of it to remind myself every time I looked in the mirror about the choices I make on a daily basis. At the time, I felt it fit best on the bridge of my back, the perfect canvas for such a defining statement. Ironically, that was one place where I'd hardly ever see it and would soon toss it aside as a meaningless mantra to trudge forward in my moments of reckless impulsion. Everything I got, I got honestly though. I was a product of my environment. I grew up on hand-me-downs and free lunch programs, but I never really wanted desperately for anything. I always said the only difference between my parents and many others was priorities. Working-class families bought material things to appease their kids when they could. Being privileged enough to sit on the bottom tier of the so-called "middle class" meant I got books and summer boarding camps, but couldn't afford other luxuries. I never appreciated it then, but I realized how much different my perspective was as I progressed through school.

Lincoln High was a small school in the backcountry town of Palmetto, South Carolina. Believe it or not, it sat on the grounds of a historic tobacco plantation, one of the wealthiest slave estates in the South up until Reconstruction. Putting a school there with a mission to increase college enrollment for one of the state's lowest performing (and predominantly minority) academic regions was an empowering idea, but the execution fell short of creating tangible opportunities for success beyond our surroundings. Harsh disciplinary practices levied against Black students made the school-to-prison pipeline an unfortunate reality for many who simply lacked confidence and guidance.

There were six degrees of separation or less that existed for students who lived in under-resourced, low-income areas like ours. I never lived in the projects, but much of my family did at some point or another, and I would frequent my cousins' places in Forest Grove while my mom was away for work. Every day, I rode the bus with the O'Clair PJ's crew and the Zoo Road gang and I laughed with the rejects and the troublemakers in school and outside of it. There were students in our school whose parents owned large businesses, who were doctors, who threw "Sweet Sixteen" parties and enabled them to rock thousands of dollars in designer fashion every day. There were also 70% of us on free and reduced lunch programs, and even more students whose aspirations and extracurriculars were often limited by financial barriers to participation. Yet, we were all united by a sobering reality of life in Sampson County where opportunities were lacking and danger was lurking around every corner. No matter who you were, one wrong move could mean a lifetime of potential cut short.

Most of us had just enough money to not need for anything, but we were all just poor enough to not be able to afford the luxuries of life. For my brothers and I, wants often waited long past our desire for them. I remember before every school year my aunt would send a bag to my grandma's house, full of passed-down clothes from my older cousins who were about two sizes bigger than I was at least. If she felt like it, my mother would take us to the big flea market in Ragsdale to buy knockoff items for cheap. I loved the lively sights and intoxicating smells of some of the South's most famous foods being sold by ambitious merchants working hard to make ends meet with their families. The enticing aroma of succulent meat skewers dripping with juices placed over hot pita and fried sweets covered in powdered sugar lingered under the haze of the giant tents. Freshly-caught seafood from right off the South Carolina coast was always in abundance. Tables lined with the finest linens, fragrances, fashion pieces, and all types of handmade products invited the eyes of passersby as merchants haggled over bargain prices. What some would consider "dirt cheap" felt like a fortune when spending our hard-earned savings, yet we indulged ourselves unabashedly and delightedly in what were then the spoils of life for a young boy in rural SC. We could never afford real $200 Jordans, Timberlands, and other popular shoes. For a fraction of the price, we bought customized knockoffs that quickly disintegrated after a couple of months under the stress of our big feet and wild ways. I didn't know it then, but I was learning important considerations for future cost-benefit analyses. Those were the days.

Have you ever been deprived of something so long that you no longer want it? I grew up not caring too much about designer brands and jewelry or the latest fads because I could never have them growing up. When my mother could afford to buy us the finer things, she spent her discretionary funds on educational opportunities for us instead. In addition to the summer camps, she afforded our participation in travel sports leagues and frequently sought learning destinations for us to vacation while exploring the wonders of the world through historical landmarks and events. We'd write book reports on the figures we'd learn about along the way and take turns reciting literature in the car to test our cultural appreciation.

As I grew older and drifted away from those moments, I would sometimes daydream about my childhood and was reminded of how hungry I used to be for adventure as a young boy, reading a new book every night by flashlight. I remember waiting until after my mother flicked the lights out and sent us to bed. As I bid her goodnight, I'd reach for a book under my pillow, anxious to get lost on a new adventure in a new world. I'd usually wake up tired and grumpy, with the book folded underneath me in the bed, blowing my cover each time. My mom would never chastise me; she just smiled and told me I'd soon be wearing glasses one day if I stayed up reading every night in the dark.

There was something magical about the escape I found in books. My first pair of spectacles led me to read even more. I figured any damage had already been done, so what could it hurt to double down? My frames were a thick, round, horn-rimmed eyesore that gave me a certain esteemed look for a young scholar. It would be years before contact lenses became mainstream. Despite the "nerd" and "geek" comments they inevitably invoked from my peers, glasses were a godsend that fueled my fascination with literature even more. Reading for me was a gateway into a new life, one far away from here. I sought comfort in foreign worlds made of words until my mind rested and my eyes would settle into submission.

I'd stay up late into the night buried in a book until living room lullabies coaxed me to sleep. I'd hear Donny Hathaway's "Someday We'll All Be Free" drifting from the radio in the living room fade into the blaring of Donald Byrd's horn as I drifted off into a deep slumber. Those were the days.

The One

Plagued by aspirations to succeed,

I bleed with despair that I may never make it, that I may
become just another "used to be,"

a tale of lost talent and wasted potential,

a mirror of the malignant forces that pillage the people
I see every time I ride those familiar streets of my
hometown,

I drop to my knees...Lord please don't abandon me,

I am the chosen one...the restless optimist whose
sanguinity rises with the morning sun.

This me wasn't meant to be, He had greater things for
me to see,

I had places to be, and with the greatest gifts He
bestowed upon me, He also equipped a strength in
me,

Misery has since made way for victory among the paths
that laid before me; I chose this one and nothing
has been the same since.

Chapter Three

I remember parts of my childhood vividly, while others are a blur of intentionally forgotten pain and broken promises. My parents were young, and ambitious, and honestly—unprepared for children, but they were both from conservative families that didn't recognize abortion as an option. Thus is the way of life in the South. Tradition demanded they do what they have to do to raise their two boys. For my mother, that meant a life of sacrifice for the sake of her children. For my father, it meant restraints on unfettered freedom to do as he pleased. We moved around a few times before resettling in the Big Apple. Soon afterwards, my parents split, and I moved with my mom and younger brother to the east side of the city, known for its high crime rate and disproportionate homeless population. The three of us shared a bunk bed in a one-bedroom apartment, my brother and I alternating turns on the top bunk.

We attended the neighborhood elementary school, Elk Ridge, a five-minute walk through the wooded path that connects the adjacent park to our school playground. Our mother still dropped us off every morning out of precaution though, and our babysitter picked us up most afternoons. Her name was Hasina, a Bangladeshi teen studying at the nearby city college. She lived with her family in an apartment on the other side of the school. My mother often worked late as a janitor at one of NYC's boutique IP firms, and so we spent many evenings learning about Bangladeshi culture, staring in awe as five people dug in and out of large bowls with only their hands— careful never to pass or eat with the left one—and counting the minutes until 8:00 when my mother would be knocking on the door to take us home.

Sometimes, on Friday nights, instead of going straight home from school, my mother would have to take us to her office to finish up while she waited for overworked associates to finish up their mountains of work that never seemed to dwindle. Occasionally, I would flip through stacks of case files on someone's desk while my mother made her way down the halls. My mother took part-time law classes during the day, and my exposure to the firm intrigued me enough to ask her all sorts of questions about motions and depositions and various legal concepts I came across in my rummaging. She never seemed to get too annoyed despite her constant scolding to make sure I left the files the way I'd found them. I think she appreciated my inquisitiveness because it gave her an opportunity to test her own knowledge from class each day without the pressure of cold calls and exams. My mind was a sponge, and I willingly soaked up the wisdom from her lessons learned as a Black woman working toward a coveted position in a firm like the one she serviced every evening. A part of learning what it would be like to reach such a pinnacle of society fascinated me to the point that all I talked about was one day becoming a lawyer myself, while another part of me was terrified to live in a world where billable hours would dictate my livelihood. I would usually fidget with random things in the offices until sleep eventually came, and I could never fight it. My brother and I would curl up on the floor or in one of the office chairs, complaining over these wasted evenings of our precious youth until we passed out from self-induced exhaustion. I remember thinking repeatedly that I never wanted to grow up and work a job that ruined Friday "fun" nights with work.

After a while, the void left from the abundance of absence gave way to a feeling of longing. For what, we weren't completely sure. The late nights at the office, the missed family gatherings from several states away, the forgone opportunities that were never recouped, the persistent fear of fatality from gang violence that precluded any feelings of security my mother could offer…each of these – along with a sudden illness that slowly took hold of her capacity – would factor into her decision to relinquish her blossoming career and take us down South, back to our roots. Our eastside apartment sat square in the middle of a constant turf war as more and more Latinos flooded into a city and borough that had historically been overwhelmingly Black.

Mara Salvatrucha ("La Mara"), or MS-13 as the world came to know it, was—at the time—a rapidly growing, vicious gang that lived up to every legend of its sheer savagery. Members carried out the cruelest acts of violence without so much as a blink of an eye, and they were infamous for celebrating their reckless audacity wherever there were witnesses who could attest to their iniquity. It was the 90s, and MS-13 was at the top of the food chain, instilling fear in anyone who dared enter their territory.

What made it worse is that for thousands of Black men like me, the world believed we were the true predators when gangs like La Mara were literally terrorizing cities across the U.S. One of my best childhood friends, a pretty, tomboyish girl named Catalina whose family had recently come from El Salvador, often talked of it like a cool clique that she would inevitably become a part of one day because of her familial ties. She was only ten years old but already understood this to be her destiny, whether she embraced it or not. We would go to the movies, to the park, and have so much fun. She gave me my first introduction to "mota," years before I was rolling joints of my own. I remember sitting beside her on the playground outside of school one day when another one of our friends appeared wide eyed and smirking, a young kid named Denny from Honduras whose smile made all the girls wild when he made a fool of someone on the soccer field. I looked in confusion as he ran up to her ear and whispered loudly, "Mata, roba, viola, controla." They laughed and dapped each other up before the three of us started discussing our plans for the coming weekend. I didn't know what it meant then, and I didn't ask. Weeks later, in perfect MS-13 fashion, there was a young Black boy found mutilated into various pieces in a trash barrel lining the path through the woods to the park. Those same words were written in graffiti alongside a picture of "la garra," symbolizing the members' demonic acts carried out with machetes and their utter disregard for human life.

That was the first time I realized that protections for Black bodies weren't asserted with the same fervor as some of our fellow American brethren. The story didn't even make it a full news cycle before it was overshadowed by other, more prominent news pertaining to our nation's ever-increasing conflicts.

That experience would dissipate the passions I had for innocent childhood activities as well as the trust I placed in integral government institutions such as school. I knew that what was supposed to be one of the safest places on Earth for a child could no longer provide the expected refuge as Black children grew older, whether outside or within its walls. In my mind, the fire that burned inside for education was inextinguishable, but the light in my eyes that shined bright in spite of my surroundings would soon go dim.

Elk Ridge was a high-performing elementary school despite its position in an area of the city that was becoming overrun with criminal activity. It had a great immersion program, allowing me to be surrounded by the culture and language of my father's family in an educational setting that laid a solid foundation for the rest of my life. It wasn't quite the Colombian slang that my grandparents used when I visited them in the Bronx, but I learned to communicate well within the blended communities of Latino immigrants that made NYC so beautiful. We had the best teachers, who, despite not looking like most of us, committed wholeheartedly to preparing us for success beyond grade school. They taught us not only how to be good students, but good citizens, and drilled into us the confidence to believe we could do and become anything in this world that we put our minds to.

I attribute much of my success in education to the foundation developed at Elk Ridge, completed by my parents' own love for lifelong learning. It was in kindergarten where I first heard that knowledge is the key to freedom. People who were quick to pick up on mine and my brother's aptitude for educational excellence never failed to tell us about the endless opportunities in store for our futures or warn us about the dangers that await those who turn to drugs or gangs for their livelihood instead of books. One of the things they forgot to mention to us, however, was that for Black boys aspiring to greatness, even when you're not dealing drugs, the outcome could likely be similar…end up dead or treated like a criminal.

My mother's family was mostly concentrated in the heart of the Lowcountry, on an old plantation that has since become known as the Sadler family farm, a landmark of the sultry southern South Carolina swampland. This was a world distinctly different from the concrete jungle my father grew up in, the land my brother and I were used to. It was a world in which my grandfather settled down after serving proudly in the nation's Air Force during the Vietnam War. He was a veteran who came from hard work and principle. His father, a Mason, passed down his traditions along with his sacred secrets and penchant for hard work. In turn, Grandfather instilled that in his six children. He was a strong, serious gentleman who knew how to make you laugh and make you cry in the same breath. Despite that disposition, he seldom employed his sternness; his presence alone commanded the respect afforded a military officer. He was charming and witty and resourceful, making wine from the grapes grown in the pasture and serving it on special occasions or finding new ways to showcase and monetize his prized farm animals at the county 4-H exhibitions.

My grandmother was a skillful, strong-willed daughter of sharecroppers whose culinary talents and green thumb were an envy for miles around. She was easygoing and had a way of making anyone feel comfortable around her. A retired schoolteacher and a seamstress, she sewed garments for people throughout the neighborhood when she wasn't leading local Girl Scouts troops on educational expeditions across the Southeast. Grandmother was the masterful matriarch of our family; the glue that kept it all together.

My mother told stories of her childhood days, including waking up at the crack of dawn with the fellow farmhands. She'd go out in the field and tend to rows of crops, lucky to beat the blistering heat from the afternoon sun. This was back-breaking work in the summer, plowing and planting and weeding and picking and shucking and snapping and canning when it's all done. In the older days, way before my time, it was expected students would miss school during harvest season to help out on the family farm. I chalked these up to be mythical tales of a time that is long gone, but in perspective, my mother was a young woman who had seen so much in a period not distantly prior to my arrival. I would soon become intimately familiar with the sentiments of students who'd wish desperately on stars to "make it" so that they'd never have to return to their family farms.

Before I left the city, I was excited and nervous to be leaving the comfort zone of the metropolis I'd known my entire life up until that point. My brother's anguish over events common to urban life compounded the ordinary problems we experienced growing up in a single-parent household and became the final straw that directed my mother to get us out of that toxic environment. She made what became a long list of sacrifices on behalf of her boys, giving up the perks and promises of her professional path to offer us a better quality of life—one surrounded by family, and fresh air, and where we could find ourselves in the natural beauty of Earth's offerings. She knew that there was nothing better in store for us here. Not now—one day when we returned as adults, maybe.

Marvin Gaye's "Inner City Blues" played like a soundtrack in my mind as I reminisced about my time in the gritty Crystal City. The final departing image of my old neighborhood, etched eternally into memory, was a sad example of the trauma that so many young, Black, gifted individuals face in pursuit of their aspirations. I flashed back to the young boy on the news outside my school, helpless and maimed. The culmination of a young life full of potential and pride in being a scholar was a startlingly brutal death sentence, which became a catalyst for the next ten years of my life. The haunting images of a school-aged boy mangled with blood matted in the curled kinks of his hair, eyes wide with terror, limbs laid apart like meat at the butcher shop, reminded me of a fate I vowed never to experience. I swore against MS-13, against the dark figures lurking in the alleyways near our old place, and against the foreign merchants who preyed on Black and Latino citizens in the very communities they set up shop in, all of them figments of a sinister way of life that I would soon be glad to depart from.

My mind drowned out the crowded thoughts of a confused child with the lyrics of a song I'd heard my mother hum from time to time. As the three of us sat cramped into a U-Haul approaching I-95 for the start of a new journey down South, James Taylor's voice came melting through the speakers, calming in its timeless melody about the prettiest place on Earth. I took one last glance at the sunshine behind the skyscrapers before drifting off to sleep, already long gone to Carolina in my mind.

Black Spots

Black spots. Black screens that shade my eyes from the
white hot of the sun but still I see black;
Black flags waving from the backs of Black brothers'
slacks,
Black sisters' black nails desperately clawing at each
other's necks, black death...
Black tears that create streaks on Black cheeks, black
streets...
The yellow line that creates division on those black
streets,
The white spots that leave stains on black sheets,
Black bottoms, shaking, moving to black beats,
Black heat brings Black screams, black dreams that are
broken...open your eyes.
Black butterflies bring rays of Black hope;
Liquid happiness that pours smoothly down Black
throats,
Black athletes blow up in clouds of black smoke, black
quotes...
Black actors, Black comedians telling black jokes, Black
progress,
Black entrepreneurs, Black shops...Black artists making
a living on backdrops,
Black hatred towards black uniforms on Black and white
cops,
Black mothers stir culinary creations in black pots, Black
faith...
Black candidates running a white race,

Lillie Lane

Black presidents bring a smile to every Black face, Black
   power…
Black clockers on the corner bidding time by the hour,
   black magic,
Black violence, black markets—white reap,
What ever happened to Black peace?

Chapter Four

started 6th grade at the neighborhood middle school, home of the Palmetto Pirates. The school was 95% African American, unlike my previous ethnically diverse elementary schools. Its history was rich with Black heroes and freedom fighters who'd go on to become key political figures, leaders of the Civil Rights movement, and exceptional educators who changed the outlook on public education in Carolina. Now, fielding pleas to close it because of its dilapidated state, PMS barely managed to maintain its student performance in line with state guidelines. This, considering being routinely ranked among the poorest school systems in the state, was Palmetto's saving grace. Cracked concrete created hazards along the breezeways between class buildings. Mold was visible in areas like the gym, where it was common to see a bucket or two catching drips from a leaky and exposed roof. Classroom walls were yellow with age instead of the pretty white seen in neighboring county schools. Boys' bathroom stalls rarely had privacy doors, and graffiti marked most of them, letting unsuspecting students know whose turf was whose.

There was always the threat of aggression if you came from the wrong side of the tracks. Rival towns sat on opposite ends of the gang spectrum; Palmetto was a Blood haven, and minutes away, Pine Bluff was Crip central. For the first time in my life, I felt neutrality wasn't an option if I wanted to flourish in this environment. I couldn't just stay out of the way; I played sports with most of the gangsters and I got all the girls, so it was inevitable that we would cross paths at some point, in some manner or another. My family—apart from the minority of educated members who'd gone on to college and found successful career paths—was entrenched in the streets, and those who affiliated themselves had major stain on the southside and westside of town. My credibility was already stamped and certified as a result. Naturally, I began to drift toward the Red Ridaz, a Billy set originating out of Broadytown a few miles away. There were others, but the 93rd ran Palmetto.

Back in those days, you could always tell who had money or a slightly more privileged upbringing by who rode the bus and who was dropped off at school. I always say that riding a public school bus builds unimaginable character. Riding the bus was torture for those who couldn't or wouldn't stand up for themselves, and Bus 187 was a living hell. I was never an aggressor, but I often held off bullies by being a comedian. My easygoing demeanor and my relatability across social groups made it easy for me to be the class clown, and I played that role to my advantage.

At the same time, I was a scholar who was constantly being invited to summer enrichment camps for the intellectually gifted and I'd scored high enough on the ACT to gain acceptance into the Early Talent Identification Program, which contributed to my advancement in invaluable ways. My teachers loathed the fact that I was often the smartest and the laziest student. Everything came easy to me, and I wasn't fazed by most of the educational challenges that came my way. I also rebelled against systems that rewarded conformity rather than unique abilities. In most senses of the word, I was a nerd—complete with subpar dress game and those same round, horn-rimmed glasses that were a staple of my childhood—yet it seems my charm and the mild cool factor that I possessed was my saving grace. I never really had problems with being bullied, but there were always people who tried me because of my laid back, friendly demeanor.

Going from our matchbox in the city to living in a single-family home with my grandparents was an experience unlike any we'd ever been accustomed to. My mom used her savings to add a wing onto my grandparents' modest, brick flat level farmhouse, and my brother and I each had our own room. We had free roam access to over 400 acres of land sprawling about the Sadler and Mapleton estates, a world of opportunity for two boys who'd been previously confined to an 800 square foot apartment. We quickly unlocked our inner wild child, staying gone for hours on end, finding one adventure after another and romping through the woods with our host of cousins. Of course, it's not like we had much choice.

There were a couple of well-known rules in communities like ours. First, you'd better make a choice—in or out, but you weren't about to be coming back and forth letting out the A/C (or the heat from the wood stove in the fall and winter months). Also, there were no streetlights in the country, so when you heard someone yell out your name down the path, you'd better be in earshot to hear it so you could have your butt in the house for supper. Schoolwork was taken seriously, as each of my mother's five sisters were teachers and thus, would make sure our assignments were done correctly. They were smart and stern and aware of the deceptive talents of determined adolescents. Don't even think about acting up in school; corporal punishment was still a thing, and within thirty minutes of any incident, one of my relatives would be at our school to tear our behinds up for showing out or disrespecting authority. My middle school principal, Mr. J.P. Tillett, was a revered educator who instilled the fear of God in many of his students with a 4x4 paddle he kept hanging up on the wall in his office. He wouldn't hesitate to use it, and he knew every child's family intimately, so there was never any objection to him swinging it. Those were minor adjustments to get used to.

Hot, home-cooked meals were a rarity before now because of my mom's schedule—and, honestly, I don't think she ever had the time to learn how to cook while she was shooting for the stars and caring for two growing boys at a relatively young age. Our diet went from fast food and my mama's staple four meals—curry chicken and Jasmine rice, hot dogs and French fries, clam chowder and grilled cheese, and lasagna—to three square meals per day of food that reminded me of the types of feasts kings would share in their castles or that Jesus would prepare for the masses.

Every morning before school, I awoke to the ambrosial aroma of the finest country cooking Carolina had to offer. Bacon, scrambled cheese eggs, hot sausage, fluffy pancakes, shrimp and grits, biscuits 'n gravy, and farm-fresh preserves were staples of my favorite breakfasts. I could always count on my grandma to put a smile on my face to start the day. We ate off the land and the fruits of our labor, so we never went hungry. Our house on Peach Street lived up to its name. We had the sweetest peaches your palate could ever taste, along with grapes, blueberries, raspberries, strawberries, and melons galore. We had vegetables in abundance. In fact, it wasn't until years later, when I went off to college, that I ever bought fruit or vegetables out of the grocery store. It became a foreign concept to me the more I was spoiled on the farm.

One of my finest memories is of my grandfather beaming from his tractor among verdant fields full of fresh produce. He paid cash for the tractor with his last check from the military upon retirement. Everything he had, he got honestly and worked tirelessly for. My grandfather instilled values in me that I revisit in certain situations to this day and taught me a lot of my early lessons in life. He took out his service dress uniform and showed me how to tie a tie and polish shoes. Grandfather talked with me about the Birds and the Bees after my first date and showed me how to make a living as a man without depending on anyone, including how to be resilient in my mistakes.

While he was usually a man of few words, and I appreciated that then, I'd later come to regret not asking and engaging him more once he was no longer around. One of the most important things I learned from my granddaddy was how to fight. He loved reflecting on the greats and how the warrior qualities of men have persisted since the early instincts of cave dwellers. When it came to boxing, Grandfather was a regular raconteur, and he could throw punches as well as he could tell stories. He could weave together words of splendor or spoil with the snap of a finger, but he always laced his anecdotes with lessons of life.

Grandfather grew up one of the youngest in a family of twelve, and so he was constantly defending himself from the antics of his older brothers. To the world, he was as mean as a snake, red and fiery in defense of himself, but really, he was just a product of his environment. His dad, my great grandfather, had been a violent drunk after escaping slavery. He had changed his last name from that of his slave master's to conceal his identity, and the hatred force-fed him during slavery revealed itself in abusive ways when he couldn't provide for his family despite everything he'd gone through.

My grandfather experienced the chilling after-effects of slavery in the form of Jim Crow laws, returning home to mistreatment and inferior conditions after nearly giving his life on behalf of a country that would seemingly never love him. His days spent amongst the rice paddies and wooded war zones of Vietnam scarred him and often brought unpleasant memories that tormented his mind. In many ways, he was misunderstood. He channeled those emotions through his hands, and though small in stature, he had fists like rock boulders. I learned my quickness and instinct from him, never dropping my guard or letting an opponent get too close without dropping the hammer. I grew up in the last days of fist fights, before children turned to guns to solve their problems. It's because of my grandfather that I've always been a brawler; a sophisticated one, nonetheless.

I was always getting into scuffles with kids from other neighborhoods who came to our court or our path without the proper deference for the Peach Tree crew. It wasn't until 6th grade at PMS that I got into my first real, adversarial fight at school, however. It was lunchtime in the cafeteria, a period of amplified aggressions between antagonists and unrestrained opportunity to act on them. We were having our usual roast session when my witty comments got the best of Rakel and drew the laughter of several nearby tables when someone repeated the burn. Not everybody could handle joanin', and he was one of them. He started running off at the mouth, threatening to "handle me" when he caught me outside of school. I knew he was light work and further antagonized him as the bell went him off, signaling next period. I wasn't threatened at all, and consequently made the mistake of turning my back on him in comfort and naivete.

As we exited the cafeteria, he smacked the back of my neck. To my surprise, there was no teacher in sight and the crowd of students separated as we started to box. I pushed him hard into the wall as he swung and missed, then my right fist connected with the square of his jaw as two teachers came running in to break us up. Apparently, I looked to be more of the aggressor because Mr. Fenty yoked me up with both arms behind my back while Ms. Armstrong attempted to grab Rake . He pushed her off and ran at me as Mr. Fenty began pulling me away, swinging around the teacher and landing a solid shot to my eye while I stood defenseless. All the kids standing in the hall went crazy with excitement, as if he'd done something worthy of applause. It was a sucker punch that swelled my eye quickly, infuriating me as I was corralled to the office. Several 7th and 8th graders passed us, pointing and whispering as they gawked at my puffy eye. It appeared as though I'd gotten my ass whooped, when really it was a lucky cheap shot that shouldn't have landed.

My mother was furious. Several weeks later, in football practice, I got into another fight with a boy named Matthew from the other side of the tracks. He was a cocky but mediocre athlete whose mouth often wrote checks his little scrawny ass couldn't cash. I decked him with my helmet, setting off a brawl between rival neighborhood players that ended in several knots on both sides and a black eye for one unsuspecting kid who'd been muddled into the melee. That was my last week at PMS. My mother thought I was out of control and needed a clean start to get my act together.

There was a new school in town that had been founded by big-time philanthropists out of New York, run by two hotshot educators who'd managed to convince hundreds of families of impoverished Black youth that they had the secret recipe to student success. It started as Lincoln Preparatory on a modest plot of land with conjoined trailers configured into bare-bones classrooms. School days started with chants and ended at 4:00pm after an intense nine-hour school day. With the beginning of 7th grade came a heightened arousal and interest in girls, and I loved the variety of options available to me at this new school.

33   Lillie Lane

Girls on my bus, in my church, in my class, and everywhere else I went seemed to have a magnetic appeal that drew all of my attention. In fact, impressing girls became central to my existence at some point and preoccupied my thoughts to the point of perversion. Elaborately folded love notes were the preferred communication channel for young girls expressing their desires in those days, and I was always amazed at the creativity of pubescent teens in their thirst for budding love. I started a collection of love notes that would grow to over 1,000 by the end of high school as I got more involved with extracurriculars and put my talents on display. I came into my own as an athlete, excelling in football, soccer, and track. My events were the shot put and discus throw, and man could I launch them. Natural, farm-cultivated strength and agility made me a threat in any competition, both regional and national. On the football field, I grew bloodthirsty and began to seek opportunities for brutalizing my opponents rather than playing for the love of the game. I was a headhunter, laying wood wherever a man dared cross my path.

I acclimated to my new school with few issues other than being too much for many of my teachers to handle. I proved them wrong about me every chance I got and ended the year on a high note by crushing the end of year exams and scoring in the 99th percentile statewide on each one. I had already been granted access to the nation's premier accelerator program for academically gifted adolescents, and now my performance afforded opportunities to attend academic summer camps across the nation. Each was stacked with elite talent, pitting me against some of the best and brightest individuals for a chance to test my mettle against the supposed ironclad intellect of students whose parents could buy their way into any college they dreamed of. It was a formidable experience for a farm boy coming from a small town in Carolina. Though I'd never had issues excelling academically, there was a different caliber of competition that raised the stakes significantly. If I could make it amongst the sons of senators, daughters of Dow-indexed Fortune 500 companies, and kids whose IQs approached 130, then I could hold my own anywhere, with anyone.

It was that confidence and capacity for success that compelled my school administration to advance me to the next grade when I reported for orientation later that summer. I'd already taken advanced math courses beyond 8th grade algebra, and I was ahead of my peers in nearly every other subject. Despite vocal dissent from one teacher in particular, who felt a clever Black boy who gave her trouble in class with his witty comments the year before was undeserving of such a privilege, I was moved to 9th grade at the brand-new expansion high school. Though I'd never had issues acing standardized assessments, this new journey would prove to be a test I wasn't entirely prepared for.

Running

One foot in front of the other,
The pitter-patter of cautious steps
Chasing promises yet fulfilled,
Heavy breaths struggling for wind,
Gasping for whiffs of crisp air gusting through the trees
as he ran,
There it was again—a wolf, lurking off in the distance,
A projection of his paranoia,
Slightly hidden in the shadows, surveying,
He kept running, heart pounding, fearing the
uncertainty of what lies ahead
But too afraid to turn back,
A howl, chilling yet telling in its cry,
Lifting the hairs on his arms and neck as he struggled to
keep his pace,
This place seemed as good as any to die…
He'd pondered this moment in his mind plenty a time,
All the while ignoring the Call of the Wild
From which he'd finally derived his purpose,
The wolf within tormented him,
Chomping at the chance to teach the lesson of good
and evil,
He steadied his breathing, kept the pace,
Charging ahead against the calamities that could curb
his victory,
Running towards destiny or away from fate,
No goalpost nor endzone in sight,
Heart sinking as he realized
He'd be running for the rest of his life.

Chapter Five

There I was. If the term "fresh meat" described high school freshmen, then I was as raw as they come. I was twelve years old in age only, but that made me a target for all of the microaggressions that persisted at the heights of secondary education. Teenagers with bad attitudes and chips on their shoulders looked at me as an easy outlet for their emotions, and teachers weren't as protective of someone who they felt didn't belong.

Since this was a new high school, they laid out the red carpet during orientation to get students excited about the upcoming year. Of course, I missed the opportunity to get acclimated to my teachers and peers as I made the late transition to high school. I came in during the first week of classes, and my first day caught me like a deer in headlights. Don't get me wrong, there was no imposter syndrome on my part nor was there a physical intimidation factor. I knew I could hold my own inside the classroom and outside of it, and while I would try to maintain a relatively low profile in my classes, I made it a point to impose my will through extracurricular activities.

My stature displayed the power of our family genetics, allowing me to compete for a Varsity spot upon arrival. My vernacular was advanced, my overall skill level was above average, and my awareness was acute enough to allow me to catch on pretty quickly if I ever found myself in over my head. While each of those was undoubtedly a blessing in my matriculation, they also created jealousy amongst insecure classmates. I got into my first high school fight within two weeks. His name was James, an arrogant, nerdy preacher's kid looking for cool points when he ran up on me in the bathroom.

His opportunism backfired and left him looking foolish. I used his face to break the paper towel dispenser.

The second fight occurred less than a month later. A known gang member had been antagonizing me at lunch for several days, until I decided that teaching him a lesson would be worth the trouble. He had nothing going for himself and allowed his anger about circumstances outside of his control to manipulate the very little potential he did have. Trey was 6'5 with a stride like a gazelle and a frame that was ripe for conditioning into an elite athlete. He was one of those kids who would always make the team, but the only time you'd see him was game time. Instead of training at practice or honing his skills, he preferred spending his time after school doing and selling drugs, hitting licks on unsuspecting old ladies, or breaking into school buildings to steal high-end computer and lab equipment.

He was a problem child by definition. Not that he was exceptionally adept at theft either, it's just that there were no cameras on most buildings in small town Carolina. Rural areas were usually behind on innovation and technology in general, but there was an honor code in place that was increasingly being circumvented by the newer generations. The community had been sucked dry by corrupt business leaders leeching off the now-abandoned dreams of hopeful emigrants. The forgotten industry promises of the struggling agricultural sector hung lifeless in the air all around, denoting life's fleeting successes. Most people around here got out of dodge the moment a halfway decent opportunity knocked on their door, and the rest made ends meet however they could. Criminal activity was constantly afoot in every corner of the community, a byproduct of hopelessness, and, ironically, a driving force of the desperation. It was that same desperation that brought the tension between Trey and me to a head.

A huge part of my introduction to high school was learning the unspoken rules of the road that many unfortunate students learned the hard way. Among the things that caught me by surprise was the territorial nature of teenagers who had nothing to their name other than bad acne and bills their parents conferred upon them in their ignorance. There were certain places you didn't sit, and certain bathrooms you just didn't visit—unless you were up for a round of "30 Seconds" at any given time. Even in Crystal City, where gang turf was life or death, I never played by anyone's rules other than my own, and there was no way I'd allow myself to spend the next four years afraid of taking a piss on the wrong hall. I'd have much bigger things to worry about, and this wouldn't be one of them.

"30 Seconds" was a direct reflection of its name, a relatively quick game of torturous pleasure derived by kids whose greatest successes in school involved terrorizing others. Whenever you walked into the bathroom, you were subject to a "call out" by anyone inside who wanted to box. For 30 seconds, two people would exchange vicious blows until the timer went off and they either shook hands or vowed revenge at a later time (usually after school or at a weekend social event). Only then were you allowed to use the bathroom in peace, and of course, there were some students who were more frequently targeted for these displays of machismo than others because of their social isolation or frail frames. Crowds of students would usually hang out in the bathrooms between class blocks as the game became more popular, and stories of brutal ass whippings made their way through the grapevines of various cliques. There were always the usual group of suspects who used the bathrooms as a means of skipping class—for sex, drug activity, or whatever other kinds of fun their teenage minds could cook up on a given day.

Trey, feared because of his gang ties, was the mastermind behind its introduction to Lincoln. I'd seen him fight, however, and knew he got away with a lot of wild, uncontrolled swings because his opponents were usually paralyzed by fear instead of focused on mechanics. After ignoring a bold challenge in the middle of the cafeteria over lunch one day, I knew my time was coming. Up until then, my size and insignificance as an underage pre-teen had allowed me to fly under the radar. I knew I couldn't run from my first 30 seconds challenge though, or I'd never live with myself, let alone be able to walk the halls peacefully as I pleased. I vividly remembered a playground bully incident back in the city as a young boy. Terrified of this mammoth of an individual and not wanting to get in trouble with my mama for fighting, I decided against confrontation and took off running full speed, looking behind me to make sure I was clear of the threat. I ran headfirst into a metal pole, knocking me unconscious as blood streamed down my face like something out of a horror movie. I was done running into objects trying to escape; I had to tackle this problem head on.

Instead of catching me in a bathroom, Trey ran into me in the woods behind the school during a clean-up day in which my environmental club facilitated a "forestry refresh" initiative to rid our campus of trash discarded in areas around the school's perimeter. Though I don't remember what he said to initiate the confrontation, I knew I was more heated than I'd ever been, and I allowed my rage to take control of my mental state. All thoughts of school sanctions or consequences at home escaped my mind, and I lunged at him in a fit of blind rage. We tussled for several seconds, fighting for control, then as our grips loosened, I ducked under a poorly thrown left hook to scoop him and drop him on the ground. I immediately seizec upon the favorable position and pounded his head with my fists for what seemed like forever until several members of our club came running in along with our advisor. All of them were in shock to see me going off and Trey laying curled up on the ground in defense. I was disgusted with myself, but even more with him for provoking me in my innocence, and I spat on him for good measure as they separated me from the altercation.

My mother heard the news of my incident at school, and although I wasn't suspended, she levied a hefty price to pay for my out-of-control behavior. Whatever bodily punishment I was expecting from Trey came from her and all of my aunts and uncles taking their turns to teach me a lesson about how to act when given a tremendous opportunity like the one I'd been blessed to receive. The following morning, on our way to school, my mama told me about a phone call she'd received from gang members vowing to exact revenge against me and threatening to come to our home.

I cried thinking about what I'd gotten my family into and what I'd do, wondering if this was the end of my innocence. It wasn't that I was afraid to die as much as it was being afraid of wasting potential…I didn't want to deliver my soul to God having not fulfilled my purpose on Earth, nor did I want to gamble with my chances of getting into those golden gates. I didn't want to leave people with love in their hearts for who I could or should have been and images in their mind about who I really was or things I really did that I never got time to pay restitution for. I didn't want to leave my problems unsolved, knowing I could have done more to resolve them. I didn't want to leave anything on the table.

Before Lincoln, I'd always been fascinated by the gang life from afar, interested in how people got tied in with these criminal organizations but never caring to know those details intimately. However, what I thought would be the start of a long war between me, Trey, and the other local Blood members became a bonding moment. Trey admired my courage to stand up to a force much stronger than I was, and he told me how much Bloods lauded bravery. He told me that brotherly love overcomes our depression and shared some of the darkest secrets of his personal life with me. What presented to the world as reckless disregard for life was really a cry for help, a manifestation of the pain he'd persevered over and over along his journey to adulthood.

His mother was on drugs, his father left when he was five, and he routinely had to find creative ways to feed his younger siblings in his parents' absence, which often meant turning to crime. He told me about his favorite subjects and how he wished he could learn more through books and travel outside of our small town but couldn't afford either, so he stole a computer to find that knowledge instead. His poor academic performance was not purely a matter of lacking competent mental abilities, but rather an intentional sabotage of success that wasn't guaranteed to people like him. No matter how well he did in school, he knew that the perils of poverty and its byproducts were a bottomless pit that most Black men never escape from. I knew then that I was in a different world. The rural South is a universe of its own in so many regards, and its effects were felt differently—often more harshly—than their equivalents in urban America. Palmetto was distinctly different in its own right, and there were many aspects of my identity that grew, while others diminished as a result.

I remember being back in Crystal City, walking past the fields after school and watching in awe as the players from the Latino League put on a show. As a boy whose first score came on a soccer field, years before I'd step onto a gridiron, seeing players from all over come and do their thing was a treat I'd never tire of. Young and old, gang members and working class alike, came together for weekend fútbol games that rivaled professional matches. They dazzled spectators with deft footwork and shouted constantly in various slang from their respective regions. I could sit for hours admiring their talent, and I took mental notes to add to my own skill set. Fútbol is a game of concentration, discipline, position, and work ethic. Each of those must combine to form a high IQ. Depending on where you are in the world, fútbol or soccer is one of those universal languages that translates across continents and cultures, and has contributed significantly to the physical and social development of so many.

On top of being great for endurance and weight loss in my transformation from husky to hunk, the game introduced me to people and took me to places that contributed to my appreciation for diversity. It was a true equalizer, a sport loved across the world.

Lincoln didn't have a soccer team initially. In fact, only two schools in the entire Sampson or its three neighboring counties did. The region was known for producing basketball and football players, and that's where most schools dumped majority of their athletic budget. However, there was a recreation league in a nearby town where the interest was high enough to warrant the facilities. My contributions on the football field afforded me special treatment from my coaches, and they let me leave practice early every day to make it to Rock Creek for soccer practice. I convinced them that it would help with my footwork and stamina. My mama or one of my aunts would show up and drive the 30 minutes to Falls River Park where we had our soccer practices and games. I got used to changing in the car coming from school during the week or church on Sundays. My brother and I had made a notable impact from the moment we moved to Palmetto and found out about the league in Rock Creek. That was the economic base of neighboring Southampton County and its only predominantly white town. As two Black boys coming from Palmetto to play, we were often the only players of color on our teams. That fueled our level of competition even more and we routinely made the all-star travel teams at the end of each season. Most people from Palmetto didn't know we played, though. It wasn't something that we necessarily kept hidden, but it also wasn't something that came up in conversations with our peers, either. There were no soccer fields out in the swamps where we lived. Many kids had never seen a soccer ball or game, partly because many parents couldn't afford to sign their kids up for recreational activities half an hour away and partly because the general consensus on soccer in Palmetto, aside from the Latino population, was "that's that white people shit."

We were already labeled the "city boys" by our family and regarded as such by our peers because of our eclectic taste in cuisine and our oddly proper pronunciation of words. Being looked at as a Yankee didn't necessarily endear you to the folks around rural Carolina, and my brother and I weren't looking for negative ways to stand out. That contributed to our desperation for a way out, whether through soccer or some other endeavor. I began to fill my free time with extracurriculars that would allow me to become more well-rounded for future opportunities, and I would look to spend nearly every summer away at summer camps to escape the farm life. Though it was majestic in many ways, the small-town life seemed to suck parts of me dry. I'd gone nearly blind reading in the dark or surfing the web for hours on end, and I saw the endless possibilities for the future of innovation. I didn't see that here on the farm. I saw the happiness it gave my grandparents, but I didn't get that same feeling, not then. What I saw instead was the writing on the walls for a dying industry and a decreasing promise of prosperity for those at the bottom of the agricultural sector. There's no way I could spend the rest of my life here digging away in the dirt at my own death.

L. O. V. E...

Love;

The manifestation of feelings indescribable by man's
tongue,

A plateau far beyond Earth's highest peaks, when we
meet...

Oh how I can't wait to taste you,

To indulge you with sweet nothings in your ear until
you can no longer stand to hold out,

Those screams inside let em' out,

Moan with the passion of a thousand slaves waiting
to break free from the shackles that constrict their
soul,

Released from initial inhibitions, let the floods of
indiscretion flow marvelously from within you,

Your temple, I kneel before you in your glory, anxious to
fill your inner pages with the story of us,

Of sacrificial lambs that become muses in the aftermath,

Factoring math into equations that turn temptations
into the sensations of sultry exchanges,

Four letters that get mo' better and mo' wetter with
every stroke of rhythm,

A system, made especially for you and I,

And when we die, let truth speak to the masses whose
minds question the depths of their own desires,

Where there's light, there's love...no feelings without
fire.

Chapter Six

Sophomore year was when I finally came into my own. I'd survived the endless jokes associated with being a pre-teen as a freshman, and I'd dealt with all the growing pains that came with high school. Lincoln was still new, but I wasn't. My reputation on the field and off was enough to be considered popular, and I enjoyed the advantages of being a trifecta of talent, intellect, and good looks. While school was otherwise successful, my academics began to slip out of focus into the background of love, lust, and longing for the privileges of adulthood. Straight A's became less of a priority as I became increasingly infatuated with the power of a woman's presence.

I had dated here and there, but only as a matter of social status. I dated girls in popular circles simply because the opportunities had presented themselves and would be a good look. There was no real pursuit. That changed when she came. When the new class arrived at Lincoln, we knew we were in for a new era. Lincoln was starting to feel like a real high school with real prospects. There were a few studs in the freshman class who were expected to take our program to the next level in SCHSAA competition. The talent certainly wasn't limited to athletics either. There was one girl, Hilda High, who took my breath away when she walked into a room. I immediately felt what it was like to lust after someone. She was pretty as magnolias in May, with long, flowing jet-black hair, a smile like Easter Sunday, and the high-cheeked facial structure of an African goddess. Her gorgeous smile lit up the hallway when she walked past, and she possessed a glow that seemed to let the world know she was a product of divine creation. We had an advanced placement chemistry class together, and I couldn't take my eyes off of her during lab exercises. Everything about her was mesmerizing, and for the first time, I was lost for words when we made eye contact with each other in passing. The shyness of social anxiety attached to the butterfly feelings of teen crushes is a fascinating segment of sociology. I relished school days for a chance to glimpse her smooth, chocolate skin and her silky hair that hung neatly down her back like a beautiful mane, sitting right above that cuff that made young hormonal boys like me willing to risk it all.

I was told at an early age that women like a man who can make them sing, and so I learned how to hold a note...to sustain it at just the right spot so that you wished it would never end. I've been in and out of choir rehearsals ever since. Duets with her were always the best too, until one day those notes didn't sound the same. We tried and tried to make music, but it just never came. I no longer felt the magic. Such is life, fleeting and unpredictable.

As the fall became winter, Hilda and I severed our teenage love affair after having only been official for a few short weeks. We went from spending countless hours after school together, her in my sweatshirts and me in her food, greedily devouring her supplies of snacks and goodies from her mother's bakery, to being strangers. Her face, still soft and calming, was once the light in my eyes on my darkest days of high school. Her gentle spirit had once mellowed my disturbed soul as I grew cold with rage. Now, I wanted nothing to do with her.

My relationship with my father was rocky at best and my home life was tumultuous. My mother never remarried but she began seeing a man who wasn't good enough for her – no one ever was, and his son who visited with him was a terrible byproduct of both of his parents' bastardization. I saw what I disliked in that dynamic, knowing that the relationships amongst my future household could never be like that. The anger of abandonment by my own father and the feeling of going without while his second family lived in splendor burned a vicious brand of hatred into my heart.

I fell into a slump and foolishly surrendered opportunities to spread my wings elsewhere when given a chance to leave Lincoln for better institutions. I had no safety net at those boarding schools, no bonding factor that linked the stories of snobby rich kids with my own. I wondered if not having or knowing a father at all was better than an absent, abusive one. Trey helped me exhale the disappointment through dank clouds of doja rolled in savory swishers, or, on good days, fat Dutch blunts that reminded us of hog legs. He wrote raps and we traded bars back and forth in fun over smoke sessions. That was my introduction to real, heartfelt writing. "Damu." Trey, Deandre, Damien, Baldy, K-wayne…through the shared pains of unfulfilled potential, they became my brothers. It was through them that I learned the street code of ethics, OMERTA, a staple of organized crime syndcates.

One brisk, winter night after basketball practice, waiting for the girls to get out so we could have some fun, the homies asked me if I finally wanted to come home. Bounty Hunters were the honchos in our hood. Any and everything ran through them, starting at the top of 112th Street on the eastside. My best friend Dee had leveled up to three stars and had significant stain on our side of town. I had put in work here and there to make ends meet or help my mom whenever her boyfriend came up short—an increasingly frequent occurrence—and had developed a trust with the set borne out of mutual respect.

There were two other cards on the scene, Billy and Don, and though they flew under the same flag generally, their principles and ways of everyday gang life were distinctly different. To get down, I would have to shoot the 31 or 47 seconds, holding my own in a circle of gangstas looking for blood. I knew I could stand ten toes with anyone and so I handled my business. When we finished, I took my shirt off in celebration under the cool night sky as I was honored with the mark of the beast: a dog paw burned into the shoulder of my right arm.

It took longer than expected to heal, and my basketball coach noticed it one day in practice. He reported me to the principal, Ms. Thieli, who told my history teacher because she knew that was the closest authority who could truly reach me at Lincoln. Ms. St-Onge was a smoking hot hippie who came from the Northeast all the way down South to teach in a rural, impoverished school district because her life passion was to make a difference. She soon learned that her passion alone was powerless against the myriad of factors facing the students in her classrooms, and that making a difference in a system set up for underprivileged minority students to fail is quite a task.

Nevertheless, she persisted in her enthusiastic attempts to transform small-town classrooms into places of historical and theatrical significance, where primitive minds came to be molded into masterful machines of innovation and social progression. She was the fantasy of my young hormonal imagination, and she had a profound effect on my appreciation for world literature. She read passages to us in class that compelled my own literary works. When she discovered my affinity for storytelling, she purchased a journal that I used to write crude poems describing the sobering realities of jobless, drug-filled communities.

Between Hilda and Ms. St-Onge, there was a barrier preventing me from breaking through the bubble and falling completely to the inviting gestures of gang influence. When they both left at the end of the year—Hilda to Houston, TX with her mother's new job and Ms. St-Onge to get her PhD after her contract expired—I didn't know if I would ever find two people from such vastly different worlds who understood me the way they did.

Weeks later, I was arrested for the first time. Four of us, all late teenage Black males with sling bags and hoodies on in the chilly weather of this vibrant mountain town, were walking down a busy street one night when we came around a corner and were ambushed by a group of police officers. They interrogated us about our parents' whereabouts and told us we were breaking the municipal curfew for adolescents, then told us we were under arrest for selling marijuana to an undercover officer. Of course, a search found small portions of the drug between us, party favors for our weeklong vacation in Santa Diabla. I remember being placed face-down on the pavement with my hands behind my back as crowds of people literally stepped over my outstretched feet along the congested sidewalk. I watched in sheer embarrassment as groups of white teenagers walked past, eating ice cream, laughing, and having fun in oblivion to the prejudices of the world. Their privilege afforded them extra consideration and freedom that we weren't privy to.

The officers lifted us from the ground by our arms and walked us to waiting patrol cars around the corner. We noticed a big school bus with barred windows that had several other teenagers, all Black and brown boys, who presumably were being charged solely with the less serious offense of curfew violation. For the less fortunate like all of us who happened to be caught in the wrong place at the wrong time, this was a swift introduction to the spiraling criminal justice system.

As they placed us in the backseat, each in a different vehicle, I asked an officer to loosen the handcuffs that had imprinted my wrists and threatened my circulation. He loosened them just enough for me to feel the numbness leave my fingers. When we arrived at Castalia County Juvenile Detention Center, we were each processed in and asked to step inside a small holding cell to be strip-searched after fingerprinting. A burly, bearded white man stood towering over me as he barked at me to bend over, hold my nuts, and cough for him. I was caught off guard and I froze, wondering if I'd heard him correctly. "You heard me. Strip…and don't take all night," he said without regard to the agonizing look of sheer terror and confusion on my face.

Those five minutes in that space will sit in the darkest corners of my mind forever, because I'd never before felt so violated. I remember us being two blocks away from our hotel at the time of our arrest, and how I'd urged us to head back an hour earlier because we'd been out all day and I was tired with body odor and aching feet. All I wanted to do was get back to Paradise Palace for a shower to regroup for the next day, our last day before departure. As I squatted, I could smell myself. The feeling was eerily similar to how my ancestors must have felt cramped in tight quarters on slave ships or standing on auction blocks as they were forced to perform humiliating tricks for traders.

We made bail a couple of days later and returned home to the East Coast. My aunt, a California attorney, got the D.A. to drop all charges without us having to return, citing invalid search and seizure, among other things that were compelling enough for them to let us off scot-free. Thankfully, we avoided a criminal record, but the trauma lingered long after that encounter.

Writing no longer served as an effective outlet for my pent-up emotions because no matter what happened, neither the words on the pages nor the creative imagination in my mind could free me from the burdens of my own captivity. Trouble found me in my most vulnerable state, and little did I know, it would follow me for years to come. My mother thought I needed a new environment and sent me away to boarding school in Greensboro, NC. A friend of hers was able to call in a favor from an old friend who got me admitted into one of the finest schools in North Carolina, where prestigious government officials and the crème de la crème of southern aristocracy sent their children. I rebelled against an opportunity for advancement, better academics, and better athletic facilities and recruitment chances. Back in rural SC, there were no scouts and very few avenues for many students after graduation from high school. Nevertheless, the appeals of opportunity at this new school didn't stop me from losing my cool when insulted with racial slurs.

One day, an overweight, pig-faced redhead boy named Scott Duncan worked up the courage to call me a nigger after being dared to say it at a lunch table full of jocks. I'd walked into the cafeteria unsuspectingly as onlookers gazed in amazement at what they thought would be quite a spectacle. Scott approached me with a smug grin on his face as he boldly parted his lips to debase my character. The word was as vile then as it had been when used against my slain ancestors swinging from Poplar trees for hundreds of years prior. I glared at him, *through* him to the glass window behind him. I envisioned myself ripping his smug face off of his fat, stumpy neck and punting it across the parking lot below. What followed should have been a cocked fist, but instead I greeted him with a cool smile and a cold, calculated response soon to come.

Known for laying wood between the lines, I knew how I'd teach this wise ass a lesson. In football practice later that day, I anxiously ran out for extra reps against the scout offense. I slid into my favorite position at the Rover and locked in on Scott in the backfield. I was the starting tailback and middle linebacker, so I knew all of the plays and formations like the back of my hand. On the very first play from scrimmage, the quarterback staggered clumsily after the snap in what was a pitiful attempt at a play action. I watched, bloodthirsty, as Scott telegraphed his steps, angling towards the guard's outside hip. The QB got nervous and handed the ball off instead of testing his arm. Wrong option. I'd started into my back pedal but came crashing downhill like a strike of lightning, viciously clenching my mouthpiece between my teeth as Scott saw his life flash before his eyes. "POW!" The sound rang out like a canon bursting across the field. I heard him wince painfully as he tried to get up. I saw that he'd bitten through his lip where his mouthpiece was missing. He was groaning and clutching his shoulder, and instantly everyone around let out a gasp. A bone protruded awkwardly from his collar, a distorted image of jersey and shoulder pads hiding the rest of the injury. He left practice with a broken clavicle. Coach called practice and made us all go home.

The next day, I was summoned to the office. They told me my time was up at Aycock Academy. I never told the headmaster about being called a nigger. Racial histories and the threat of unrest ran deep around here. After all, in states within the Bible Belt, this type of privileged prejudice was nearly as common as hellos from every passerby, though slightly more subtle in civil times. There had been a riot over a police shooting months earlier, and times weren't exactly civil.

That night my aunt, who lived locally, told me I'd be enrolling in a nearby public high school the next day and insisted I allow her husband to cut my hair so I'd be presentable on my first day. Her husband, an old, retired barber whose hands shook when he talked, ended up ruining my request for a crisp taper and left me looking like I'd cut my own hair without a mirror in sight.

Dudley High School had a reputation for its diversity, size, and dominance in nearly everything. I took my flag with me just in case I needed to hide my hideous haircut with a bandanna. I'd made it through third period when I could no longer stomach the stares or pointed laughs as people acknowledged the new guy with the tragic fade. I donned my bandanna in an elegant fashion, wrapped around my head like a headband rather than covering it completely, and yet, I was met by the vice principal in the hallways between 4th period and lunch to escort me to the office. I was dismissed from school at 2:00 pm for inciting gang activity. Some fashion statement. By 4:30 pm, I was on a bus with all of my bags headed back to the Lowcountry of SC.

I'd missed so many days between the two schools that after skipping several grades previously, I was now repeating one. The next two years flew by as I repeated tenth grade and skated through junior year with relatively no issues. Only, there was a reckoning I'd yet to come to terms with that I needed to learn before stepping foot out into the real world on my own.

Imagine

Atmospheres beyond measures,

I'm light years away from your nearest perception of
reality,

Metaphoric catastrophes sporadically create havoc in
each of our own lives,

Rewriting fate with each turn of the page, each passing
of day

Brings with it an abundance of regeneration that is life;

A slow dissipation of your being but with meaning,

And feelings, and cycles,

Siphoning every drop of individuality that is you and
replacing it with an object as we progress,

I digress…

Me? What insurmountable feats have I overcome to
make it this far, and how?

The questions of life that linger long past their welcome
–

Creating cocktails of confusion that intoxicate us with
the poisons of uncertainty and doubt,

Ambivalent statements clouded by unequivocal events
ensure that no one will ever figure it out;

Those dreams that become manifestations of an
eminent purpose,

The soulful yearning of a mere sip from life's chalice of
pleasures, ahh…yes, this is me,

These are the riches which with great fervor I seek,

Cloaked in the secure veil of comfort,

Aligned with the ideals of bureaucratic agendas and
capitalistic welfare,

America the free…oh, my country 'tis of thee, of thee I
surely sing,
To whom do I owe the extension of my gratitude?
Many men set out upon this race, and all with notions to
be anything but nothing,
And so it was with me—internalized and a seed
secreted,
But who would imagine such a King?

Lillie Lane

Chapter Seven

At Aycock, they'd called me nigger so often that I found myself in the twilight zone every day, wondering if this was how my ancestors felt during the busing era when integration was forced down the throats of white Southerners. They reminded me that the school, named after prominent segregationist Charles B. Aycock, was theirs and not mine, and that no matter how many individual battles I won, I couldn't kick everyone's ass or escape their vitriol day in and day out. It got to the point where I skipped school as often as I went, and when I decided I'd stop going altogether, the headmaster had me arrested. School officials, unconcerned with backlash over a problem student, had apparently held a meeting and collectively decided that if I wouldn't go voluntarily, they were going to force me. Apparently, they thought that being taken to school in handcuffs would scare me straight after an encounter with our friendly officers of the law, but their faith in local law enforcement and its "protect and serve" motto was misguided.

That morning, an SRO came into my room in the boys' wing of our co-ed housing quarters. He was accompanied by the headmaster, who I assume had joined partly for his own satisfaction and partly to ensure there was no escalation of this approach. The officer quickly put me in handcuffs after I refused once more to go to school on my own accord, and, before escorting me to the patrol car, assured the headmaster that he'd make sure I made it to school safely. The officer's eyes then turned dark at his apparent recognition of me, the glint in them a telling sign of this coincidental encounter. He said nothing most of the ride, but I knew he was the same gentleman who'd yelled at me and a group of friends earlier in the year when we were caught out late trick or treating with his lily-white daughters They were cheerleaders (one of them an heiress of the Pride of the Confederacy) at rival Mendenhall Creek and hung out with some of the guys on our team often.

As he let me out and removed the cuffs from my wrist, he said, "Boy, you don't know how good you got it at this little fancy school…I suggest you get your education before you end up out here with me in the real world, where we don't show any mercy."

I could feel the vitriol spewing from his lips as "boy" brought to mind images of Jim Crow that had long been erased from history books. The war on Critical Race Theory took care of that. What was otherwise candid advice possessed a racist undertone that I never forgot. I remember calling my father for his help, only to be admonished for not acquiescing to the protocol of decorum at this new school. In so many words, he suggested that I was more than deserving of whatever happened to me as a result. I knew then that my father had given up any hope he had in my future and now saw me in the same light as the men who'd just ruined my academic career, as nothing more than a delinquent. His failure to recognize the undercurrent with which such extreme and detrimental actions had been taken was fixated upon a false trust in police culture as a corrective measure for Black boys. It would be years before I'd ever forgive him for his naivete. His own privilege had seemingly blinded him from the realities of race in America, but that day—and every day thereafter for me—was a constant reminder of what still was and would be for a very long time. To my surprise, I would deal with a similar incident my final year at Lincoln.

Back at Lincoln, I was poised for one final breakout season to set the tone for my transition to the next level.

I'd already committed to Suwannee State University, a powerhouse historically Black college/university (HBCU) down in the Gullah. The first day back at school was always a movie. Those Lowcountry summertime vibes had everyone on a high. Everyone was anxious to show off their new drip, see who was new and cute, and rekindle the timeless bonds that would soon dissipate upon our graduation into adulthood. The fever that accompanied teenage boys as they chased after girls provided the most entertainment of all. Girls found out early in the high school experience that they could manipulate high school boys with their bodies and have men of all ages thirsting like rabid dogs over a piece of their flesh. It was sometimes sickening to be amongst this hunting grounds of sorts, a breeding source of broken esteem and flawed perceptions of love.

Desperate to escape the chase and settle down with one girl who would keep me focused through the business of senior year, I met a transfer who changed my world and made me reconsider leaving home for somewhere far away. Her name was Lindsay, and though she wasn't the first white girl I'd brought home to meet my family, she was the most special and the one whom I'd considered myself most serious about. She was a writer like me, and for her birthday I got her a purple diary for her to confide in and express her deepest thoughts. She'd left her bookbag in my locker one day, rushing between classes, and I decided to take a quick glance into her diary to see if there was anything in there about me.

"So, I met this boy. His name is Kameron. Everyone calls him Kibbles, like the dog food, but I like to call him KC. His family calls him King, but I think that's rather pretentious. He's tall, with superhero-like muscles bursting from every inch of his physique. He's sweet, funny, and charming enough to talk a nun out of her sacred garments. He's also brilliant; I've never met someone who *makes being smart look so effortless…and he has the prettiest brown eyes that seem to mask an unspeakable pain burning behind them. I wish I could help him put out that fire."*

She read me like a book. I never studied; coursework came easy to me. I remember countless times waking up from my naps in class to a teacher berating me and firing off questions as if to embarrass me for being asleep when I should be paying attention. I always knew the answer, though; they could never catch me slipping and I think a part of me took pride in that. My school had a culture of humiliating students who went against the grain, or who couldn't keep up with the others, or who simply had behavioral issues for one reason or another. At times, it made me sick to my stomach. Most other times, I laughed along with the other students and saved my energy to fight other battles—on the football field.

A few nights later, Lindsay's father found the entries in her diary along with a picture of me that had been stapled to one of the folded pages. He turned red with fire. He waited for her to get home from softball practice, all the while his anger brewing over as his blood became saturated by corn liquor. The moonshine enhanced his rage as he sat by the front door, pint jar in one hand and a thick leather belt in the other.

When Lindsay walked through the door she barely had time to speak before her "hey daddy" was abruptly cut off with a hard smack to the jaw. The jar in her father's hand, now of little importance, came crashing to the floor as he laid into her with all of his drunken rage. Her pale white skin began to turn purple with bruises as he struck her repeatedly, attempting to beat the God-given sense back into her that she'd apparently lost along the way. Surely this church-going gal whose daddy was a devout Deacon knew better; Southern White Christian women had no business dealing with men like me. Somehow our school, as integrated as it was, had led her to believe we now lived in a post-racial society and color didn't matter, or maybe in her teenage defiance she just didn't care for antiquated rules about Southern politics, but whatever the case, she paid a painful price for her foolish naivete.

Before storming out of the house, Lindsay's father forced her to dial my number and listen horrifyingly as he left chilling threats about what he'd do to me if he ever caught me near his daughter again. The next morning, Lindsay had been disenrolled from our school and sent to a private Christian academy one county over. That was the last I saw or heard of her.

Racial tensions in the South weren't high in these times, relatively speaking, but interracial mixing was still frowned upon in private by many households throughout the former Confederacy. Before Emmitt Till, there was Willie James Howard (born July 13, 1928), a fifteen-year-old living in Live Oak, Florida, not too far from the site of the Rosewood race massacre several years before. He was killed for allegedly writing a letter to a white girl. The girl's father found the letter and he and his accomplices went to Willie's home and ripped the young boy from his sobbing mother at gunpoint. The men picked up Willie's father where he worked and then drove to the Suwannee River. Once there, they bound Willie by the hands and feet and forced him to choose between getting shot or jumping into the Suwannee River. After his father said he could do nothing to save him, Willie jumped into the river and drowned. There was a federal investigation, but of course, no convictions followed. I knew I couldn't bear to end up the same way, so I vowed never to fall for a white woman again.

By January, "senioritis" was in full effect and as a soon-to-be-liberated teenager, I was smelling myself big time. On the morning of yearbook pictures, my mama asked me to do something, knowing I was already late for school. I was on my phone arranging club meet-ups for group photos, only halfway paying attention, and her patience had already been worn thin by my hard-headed brother. "KC, what are you doing?! Do you hear me talking to you? Get off your damn phone and do what I asked so I can get everyone in this house where they need to be!"

My reply was, "Ma, it's called an iPhone...which means whatever I'm doing over here has nothing to do with YOU."

I awoke the next morning with a headache and a sore backside. It was the first time I believed wholeheartedly that my mother could actually "knock me into next week" as my elders so often threatened whenever I would act out. However, I also awoke with a level of clarity I hadn't felt in a while. I realized that with only a few months left in my high school experience, it was time to really prepare for the road ahead. I had been so consumed with fanciful thoughts of who/what I would be and poorly planned long-term goals that, at the moment, amounted to nothing more than wishful thinking. It was time to lock in and get focused on my future.

A dream is but a thing, just an imaginative thought until time, together with action, transforms it from mind into matter. It was time to get to work manifesting the mountaintop of success I aspired to in my future.

Becoming

I am me. Indeed....

Beautifully unique despite our shared interests and
history,

A construct whose worth is dictated not by superficial
societal conventions,

But rather the culmination of creative brilliance
endorsed by the Creator himself,

I am top shelf...

I am excellence and emotion in human form,

A black unicorn–

The gift I've been awaiting all along was right before
me,

Within me, inherent in the essence of my existence,

Forgive me for the riches I used to seek, my fascination
with the streets, and the idea that power is the
derivative of financial prosperity...

Eyes to Jah, "Coo yah, creation stepper,"

The Universe acknowledges my sincerity and provides
clarity for my convictions,

These prescriptions ought not be uniform because
the symptoms were each rooted from a different
stimulus,

Those inscriptions become destructive descriptions
when interpreted by those with devilish tongues,

I am we but I am one,

Shining bright, illuminating light like the sun,

Lost in flight, flowing like water as I run,

Indulging the curiosity of my encounters,

Blossoming flowers pass, then return like the hours as
    time is devoured,
Shifting the storms as rain showers soak the blood-
    dried earth beneath our feet.

Chapter Eight

grew up as affirmative action was ending. That period of American history, albeit brief, had done little to move the needle in minority admissions, but as the Black community knows all too well, incremental progress is still progress. As if book bans weren't enough, conservative legislatures across the southeast were making waves with one educational atrocity after another, riding the heels of the High Court's dismantling of affirmative action. Grass roots coalitions rallied to strategize new avenues to get diverse students through the doors into institutions that could no longer attempt to balance the scale for historically-marginalized applicants in the same way. When it became clear that legacy admissions did not work to the advantage of minority applicants in the same way that those same processes aided their white counterparts, competitive leverage was found in the least likely of places.

Geography became an advantage in rural, underserved areas where it was largely seen as a hindrance before. Signs of an 'awakening' years in the making pointed to school funding formulas and the de facto segregation that dominated the South. Now, the bigger the playing field and more resources in the district, the worse your chances as a Black or brown applicant aiming for admission into elite universities. Students from Title I districts like mine excelling against relatively mediocre competition were diamonds in the rough. These scholars could basically write their entry tickets in large part because of their home zip code. It was seemingly a comparative analysis of "look what I did coming from where I am," and being a big fish from a small pond took the trophy every time.

That summer before I left for SSU, time seemed to slow down. Trips to Stallings Island gave me glowing brown skin as I sat for hours in the sun, dreaming about who I might be someday. I spent long days in the marshes passing time the way every Lowcountry kid knew best, frog gigging and gator spooking. There was an annual competition every summer that would pit the local high school graduates against each other in an effort to feed charities and raise scholarship funds. Whoever caught the biggest bullfrog would receive $500 toward their college expenses and their family would have bragging rights for the year, including a picture hung at the "Croakin' Toad," a popular dive bar near the Marsh Battery. The catch would be distributed amongst needy families in nearby Charleston County.

When I wasn't knee deep in pluff mud, I was usually with one of my close cousins or my homie Tony. Tony and I had attended Lincoln together for a while until he started making "real money" and dropped out. He had stories for days to keep anyone laughing, but his great sense of humor was overshadowed by an affinity for misdeeds and his reputation as a known drug dealer. Tony was bad news. He would step on motherfuckers like he stepped on the cocaine and heroin he flooded impoverished neighborhoods with. Both of Tony's parents struggled with addiction and homelessness, and he was on a warpath to avenge their failures by any means necessary. Drugs were easily accessible and, naturally, became his calling. He had no problem polluting the supply—to the detriment of his own people nonetheless—for the sake of stretching a few more knots out the pot.

Tony wasn't the only one who excelled in misdeeds. I had no shortage of troublemaking companions. Like Tony, though. I only hung out with and placed my trust in those I could count on for loyalty, without condition. Two-legged or four-legged, it didn't matter. In fact, some of my closest confidantes resided right there on the farm.

Our beloved family dog, Buster, was a farmer's dog if I've ever seen one. He lived a life of luxury, roaming the nearly 400-acre estate as if he owned every inch of it, and returning home just in time each day for suppertime. He was a lazy dog generally, but especially during the summer months. He had a favorite spot in prime view of the action on the rest of the farm; usually he was found estivating under the big old oak tree at the top of the hill, avoiding the scorching sun. He had an intolerable affinity for chasing chickens though, and as much as my grandfather loved Buster, there was no way he was going to let a dog interfere with his livelihood.

One sunny afternoon, my grandfather came in the house livid, cursing and carrying on about "that damn dog this" and "that damn dog that." Buster had gotten into the chicken coop again and I ran outside to see Grandpa's prized rooster dangling from Buster's mouth, bright crimson blood dripping onto the grass beneath him. My grandfather came back outside with his 12-gauge shotgun in hand, and I heard the slide rack quickly as he loaded a shell and raised the barrel until it was pointing directly at the dog's head. The first shot sent Buster squealing in shock, his eyes white with terror, and the second laid him down without any more fight. He was gone. My brother and I burst into tears, having watched the whole ordeal firsthand, traumatized by the sight of our favorite summer companion laying there lifeless in the dirt. As he headed back into the house, my grandfather offered the only words of consolation that you could ever expect from a man with his rationale. "Animals are property, son, not family...when it affects your livelihood, it's got to go."

When I stepped foot on campus for the first time, there was something magical that overcame me. I had been on the campus several times before, but now it felt like an extension of home. In that moment, I was where I was meant to be... where I needed to be. I couldn't begin to imagine the type of growth that would take place over the next few years as I survived one college experience after another. Persevering through the bludgeoning of chance and choice was perhaps a punishment too painful for some after escaping the realities of life where they hailed. For others like me, it was an opportunity to embrace all of the unexpected twists and turns that life has to offer. My first night in my new dorm, the infamous Scott Hall was an indication of just how wild the ride would be.

I checked into my room and got everything set up before catching a quick nap to recharge for the freshman social later that evening. I broke out my best cologne, the kind old men wear in church that you can smell three rows back. One of my best friends from high school decided to enroll at SSU as well, at the last minute, and I was grateful to have a wingman to navigate these next few years with. He lived on the other side of our dormitory, in Scott B, and I knew he would have plenty of pregame festivities to get the party started for our first night free as liberated adults. As I departed my room, I heard loud music coming from one of the suites at the end of the hall. Seconds later, three football players emerged carrying a half-naked girl on their shoulders with cans of whipped cream in each hand. I didn't realize it then, but this was a signature move of one of our campus fraternities.

As I trekked across campus, I heard the voice of my paternal grandfather warning me in my ear, urging me to be on my best behavior no matter how crazy my surroundings became. He had so many euphemisms and catchy little phrases for practically any situation. When the realization came early on in life that I was likely going to be a troublemaker because of my quick wit, disregard for authority, and my penchant for making unsavory acquaintances, it was my grandfather who would provide an understanding ear. After all, he'd gotten into his own fair share of trouble over the years. He'd always tell me, "Boy, if you can't be good, just be careful, hear?" I'd nod with a mischievous grin and go on about my way.

The first house party of the year was one for the books. Hundreds of newly emancipated young adults packed into a two-story frat house off Dewey Street, right around the corner from our university's football stadium. Smoke clouded the air inside and sweat began pouring from foreheads and armpits within minutes of entering. We were like sardines contained by the atmosphere of what would prove to be a truly epic night.

The energy was electric. I watched in amazement as the Greeks strolled through the party with their colorful paraphernalia. I noticed the way the Nupes in particular commanded the room, the swagger they possessed as they floated through the crowd, shaking their shoulders as women fell victim to the seduction of their shimmy. I was mesmerized, until someone caught my attention out of the corner of my eye. A young woman with long, flowing locs, dancing by herself in a patterned romper without seemingly a care in the world, lit up the corner of the room she was in. A sudden urge came over me and I knew that I couldn't let the opportunity go by to introduce myself. I approached her, asking her name, her classification, and where she was from. I was pleasantly surprised to hear of her New Orleans origins, as the kinship of our Creole culture provided a point of relatability that would endear us to each other as our conversations grew more frequent. The resulting connection was one that was transformational.

Her name was Joanne, but everyone on campus would soon know her as Jojo. I called her my Bajan beauty. She was the first woman I'd met outside of SC who could speak my language. I'd never heard it sound quite so beautiful as it did coming from her lips. She uttered a few words of Tut as a way of sharing a secret in a public moment of intimacy, and my eyes widened as I realized the familiarity of the language.

Tutnese is an 18th century slave language developed for secret communication and teaching purposes during a period when Black folks were unable to read or write. Though previously clandestine for obvious reasons, it has since been passed on orally through generations of African American descendants of slaves, with three distinct dialects by region. Those who hailed from the south were believed to speak the purest form of Tut, as that region produced the richest ties to its roots. I'd picked it up listening to the conversations of my grandmother when she was in earshot of children who she didn't want minding grown folks' business. It required painstaking attention to detail in order to decipher the puzzling sounds at first, but I was proud to be connected to my ancestors in some way with what had now become a dead language. Tut consists of spelling words using their phonetic sounds, with vowels pronounced normally and consonants replaced with matching syllables. *Per*, *com*, and *que/kway* would mark periods, commas, or question marks, and double letters would include the prefix *squa* or *squat* (in the case of double vowels).

"Cutohmume waxituthash mume." *Come with me*. Her voice melted like honey into the room when she talked. I felt the atmosphere shift in her presence. Her mocha skin provided a muse for my most coveted works of art, her Blackness radiating the inner light of our ancestors. From her crown to her base, she was as flawless a creation as I'd ever seen. Jojo was the epitome of grace, bestowed with a gift that made men fall at her feet in adoration. Her smile, her charm, her way of acknowledging everyone she came across in a way that made them feel seen was enchanting. For me, however, what she offered was a refuge from the storms that awaited on the horizon.

That night after the party, as hordes of students made their way towards campus through the adjacent neighborhoods, reality hit again. Two officers cut off the path of the group I was walking with and demanded we show identification. They then asked if we had any illegal substances in our possession and attempted to frisk us, capitalizing on our ignorance of the nonexistent stop-and-frisk laws in our state. It was the way of life for partygoers at SSU; our parties were always shut down early and our students' livelihoods were constantly threatened by the heightened vigilance of patrol units whose heavy presence brought with it a disproportionate level of aggression. There were six colleges and universities in the city, all within about five miles of each other, but there was only one campus that was predominantly Black. That was SSU, and that was where the local police departments spent most of their time. They patrolled our side of town, roamed our eastside neighborhoods menacingly, and offered us a constant reminder of the inequities that exist even among institutions of higher learning. The policing in Black college neighborhoods versus white neighborhoods and the targeting of Black students proved that no matter where I went, discrimination would surely follow in some form or another.

As the first semester of college came to a close, I was blindsided by the inevitable but unpredictable realization that life is far more transient than we ever imagined. The people we'd always taken for granted as being constants in our lives would depart on their own time, often without a word of warning. It was a tough pill to swallow.

Even tougher was the fact that my grandfather had guided me through some of my most precious moments thus far, and along the way, had taught me some of life's most valuable lessons. I remember finding out he was sick, only to see him still get up early every morning and toil through the day without complaint. I laughed when he would sometimes act weird, not knowing the implications of his actions or how little time I had left with him. To me, he was invincible; he had survived much, much worse, so I didn't think much of the bad days. To me, he'd bounce back and keep on going, like he'd always done throughout his life. He was my daily reminder that hard work pays off, even when you stumble multiple times along that path to success. He was the rock that cemented the foundation my grandmother had set for our family, and now he was gone.

I ended up taking exams early and heading home to spend time with my family in this period of loss. The strength of my grandmother in managing the affairs of his homegoing was inspiring and reassuring. I knew that because of who and what I came from, I was powerful beyond measure. There was no obstacle nor ordeal too great for me to persist.

His transition was beautiful. My grandfather laid there poised and presentable like the military man he was. I fought through sobs and streams of tears as my cousins and I sang a song in his honor, sending him off the way my grandmother knew he'd want to go. From his days growing up on his parents' farm to owning one of his own that would forever feed future generations of this family, my grandfather had labored incessantly and selflessly on each of our behalf. Now, he was finally at rest. Jojo sat towards the back of the church, crying along with me, understanding the significance of this moment as she had just lost her only grandfather a year prior. Her presence brought me peace, and we leaned on each other for support in the coming months. Whether she knew it or not, Jojo was an angel who'd been sent down to watch over me through this phase of my life. There is no gift nor number of words that could ever express to her the depths of my gratitude.

Who Am I?

Don't ask me who I am; ask me who I aspire to be—
Who I am now does not define me, it is not my I.D.
But yet a hopeful mirage masking this painful reality,
That I am just a mere student on the verge of insanity,
A fractional being struggling to achieve the American
     dream though it seems I'll never obtain it,
So in the meantime I find a job, a piece of happiness and
     sustain it,
But no...this isn't nor will it ever be enough for me,
I see the lives of those more privileged than me and
     fiend for it constantly,
Like so many of my peers I am lost—
Oblivious to a world beyond that which is seen,
I imagine a life like this forever and I scream...
Like suspended sentences my mind is caught in
     between,
Do I remain patient for my blessing or do whatever it
     takes to succeed, even if it means being untrue to
     what makes me, me?
...But who AM I? That's the wrong question, for you see...
I do not yet know who I am and therefore cannot answer
     your question in its entirety,
I can tell you from whence derives my notoriety...I
     occupy the body of a soul who knows no fear,
Who disregards the law and keeps trouble near,
I am the underdog who struts like a champion,
I am the prisoner who shall not perish, he who walks
     toward death with his head held high,
Who looks fate in the eye and dares it to try,

I am the hope for the future, the poster child for my
peers,
I am the face of oppression, its bucket of tears,
I am a picture of prosperity, I am the voice of the poor,
I am the ear for the faint sounds of opportunity knocking
at every door,
I am the food for the famished, the essence of my
dreams,
I am what my ancestors were; I am a product of Kings—
I am all of those things, but I am still searching,
I do not yet know exactly who I am and therefore cannot
answer your question in its entirety,
So please...do not ask me who I am, but rather, who I
aspire to be.

Chapter Nine

School was out and my first summer as an adult was in. I'd turned eighteen last fall, while undertaking the gauntlet of freshman year. After surviving through the excruciating experience of shared living quarters, replete with amenities in disrepair, a vile bathroom, and irresponsible roommate, it was time for my first apartment. I'd always been reasonably responsible and unafraid of new challenges, so this one was no different. Since I was now managing all of my own affairs, it was only right that I took the initiative to place myself in a more comfortable situation, at least so I thought.

None of my close friends were ready to move on campus yet, but I needed a level of privacy that I couldn't get in a dorm room, and so I was placed randomly in a unit with two other students. That decision would forever change my life. What began as a brief reprieve from the annoyances of campus student housing quickly devolved into a chaotic environment of self-destruction. College and its cohabitation with the surrounding communities, for better or for worse, offered no shortage of opportunity for unscrupulous behavior unbecoming of academics and aspiring professional leaders. Yet, it was just this type of activity that built character and resilience into ambitious youth on a paper chase for their respective degrees.

Like so many others who shared my background and upbringing, I internalized every mistake and misstep from my past and carried it with me. My self-pity kept me oblivious to the fact that the only reason this chip on my shoulder presented as a permanent scarlet letter is because I would allow the past to reintroduce its presence with each passing encounter. Wearing that pain on my sleeve ensured its visibility, even when those around me were completely ignorant to the circumstances that had brought me to this current state. I masked my emotions with marijuana, concealed my insecurities with cocaine, poured alcohol down my throat to wash away the tears inside, and mixed it all with pills to drown out the anxiety I felt knowing that if I didn't get a handle on my habits, I'd be destined for failure. While my personal failure wouldn't necessarily equate to my family's failure, for others this was absolutely the case and the thought of their own demise carried an even heavier burden. I acknowledged and respected that fact.

My first encounter with drugs was at eleven or twelve years old. Over time, the availability and potency of drugs increased and the amount of discretion with which people consumed them decreased. The reasons for drug use are varied, though performance enhancement, social pressure, and escape from reality headline the list. The ever-changing demands of society maintained one constant; to be Black and successful in America came with a steep price that was due every day of the week, consistently placing one in the crosshairs of the status quo with relatively little refuge. To be on constant guard against the demands that we be twice as good, work twice as hard, all for seemingly half the benefit, was maddening at times.

Black students faced mounting pressures and realities that many of their classroom peers would never know or begin to empathize with, and this toll was taxing on even the most prepared or the strongest-willed. The relevant data is ripe with evidence of the byproducts of academic, economic, and social stressors, including the alarming suicide rates among students seeking terminal degrees and the PTSD exhibited by students who grow up in both urban and rural ghettos. The effects of stress are no different in Black bodies than others, however, and the manifestation of these stressors was often a driving force for the euphoria-inducing, reality-altering drug experiences that could end up ruining the lives of innocent youth.

Despite all of its promise, D.A.R.E. did little to curb the pandemic of widespread drug use. If anything, it accelerated and amplified the problem by compelling young stoners to be stealthier in their efforts. Teens were finding and using at increasing rates on through adulthood, steadily expanding their capacities as functioning addicts. Hailed as the adolescent intervention and drug prevention program of the 80s and 90s, much of its success can be attributed to the enlarged presence and aggravated aggression of police forces across the country, who used America's war on drugs as excuses to target marginalized populations. Otherwise, it was an utterly useless attempt by the government to advance an agenda it truly had no grasp of. President Reagan's "Drug Abuse Resistance Education" initiative formed as part of the nationwide "Just Say NO" campaign and boasted a $750 million annual budget allocation with little to no positive results related to drug consumption or self-esteem. In fact, the incessant pandering by police officers to curious kids highlighting drugs' taboo status actually led to further glorification and proliferation of these inhibitive products.

While the general consensus of society remains that most drugs are bad, it's harder to accept this as an unequivocal truth the more you realize that everyone around you— especially those espousing and enforcing these very policies or benefitting from them in some regard—is partaking in some manner. Everyone has their drug of choice, and it is with this nugget of enlightenment that the masses have found enjoyment in their own vices.

Even in an impaired state, I was still able to hold my own and I remained among the most competent in any of my classes, which only fueled the fire that would eventually take hold of my life. Marijuana became mushrooms, cocaine became MDMA, liquor became lean, and Xanax became ecstasy or whatever else was in rotation at the time. My class attendance began to suffer tremendously, as did my grades. I lost jobs where I was a valued employee because I could no longer make it to work on time, or, when I did, my mind was so far gone after the next fix that it was as if I wasn't there.

What broke my heart even more is that my younger brother, an Irish twin, who was much more astute and capable than me (he'd already mastered organic chemistry and been building prosthetics since he was in middle school), was following in my footsteps and quickly becoming more entrenched in the drug lifestyle than I could ever have imagined. In the wake of my destruction was a vacuum that sucked him in almost against his will, leaving him caught up in messes I'd created but without the circle of protection I'd established for myself. When he was taken away for the first time, I placed the blame squarely on my shoulders and suffered internally for months, which slowly turned into years. First-time offenders often got a different shake depending on demographics, and a young Black male was typically given anything but the benefit of the doubt. The school-to-prison pipeline was a hidden reality that tormented so many families with promising futures who found their backs pinned between shortsighted policy and the blue wall.

When Israel, my youngest brother, came into the world, those concerns were only magnified. Growing up as the oldest of three boys, navigating obstacles without much guidance and being overly adamant about doing things my way was one hell of a lesson, if not a life sentence. The fire and rain that pained my efforts consistently crippled me to the point that I eventually became numb. My life was put on autopilot for a period of time in which it seemed the only destination I was headed for was destruction, and I had a first-class ticket.

I lived in what has affectionately become known as "the trap." It lived up to every definition of its name, as evidenced by the ne'er-do-wells who walked in and out of its doors throughout the day and night, filling their bodies with the poisons of their respective vices. We existed as little more than sitting ducks, waiting directly in the line of fire for life's targeted vengeance. Frequent jail visits, drugs, and juggling women who were no good for me exacerbated the effects of existing in a toxic environment. I couldn't get out of my own way, and there was no one rushing to my rescue.

My mother was hundreds of miles away, dealing with the despair of losing her son and best friend in a tragic twist of fate. My closest brother was locked away in a cold, hard cell, tormented daily by the scoundrels of men who viewed incarceration as a way of life. He was the beloved knee baby, an unsuspecting victim of the criminal justice system; a brilliant 4.0 student who made the mistake of briefly succumbing to the pressures of being poor in a place of desperation. He was supposed to be a doctor, like I was aspiring to, but all of our dreams and plans together were taken away in the blink of an eye one warm summer night.

Though no one ever told me directly, I knew I was letting so many down who believed in me. The guilt ate at me inside. I felt my life spiraling out of control when I was dismissed from the football team in the fall of my second year pending drug counseling sessions, leaving my head spinning with questions about what was next. Little did I know, my cousin was about to provide a resort that was too hard to pass up.

Open Caskets

I had ambitions for my brother to be 6 feet,

But the idea of him being underground just missed me,

Another kiss from the reaper, no keepers, Cries comforted by the lullabies that emit from our speakers,

We till until our time has come,

Just a lease on life until the deal is closed,

Rising sun and falling stars highlight the transition of souls transposed,

From earthly elements to the heavenly realm and in between,

Careening towards fate,

Catastrophe or naturally, on display for the world to see,

In living color, from one to another,

We praise the passage of pain and cherish the day we meet again.

Chapter Ten

Counseling was short-lived. My cousin was a nationally ranked football standout at another HBCU in Florida, down there in gator country. He knew about the swamp life, and though he wasn't from the Lowcountry we always vibed whenever we linked. The mode de vie was relatable between our two homes and the bloodline was strong. He had just entered the transfer portal at the end of last season and landed at FACU, a school with a storied program and a long-established winning culture. He called me with an offer to try out for the team as a walk-on, having to earn any spot I'd eventually receive. I'd grown tired of spinning my wheels at SSU. I deserved a second chance and I owed it to more than myself to shoot my shot at a new university. This was an opportunity to set the tone for the next phase of life. I couldn't wait to see what this new scene had to offer.

A few weeks before I left for training camp, my mind was clouded with thoughts of inadequacy and uncertainty, and something kept urging me to head to our family cemetery for the answers. Every time I visited the gravesite of my grandfather I was invigorated with a sense of pride, honor, and courage to fight for the ideals I held dearest to my heart. The sadness would quickly give way to a different sensation, however. My soul was saturated with a sense of purpose, and I was determined to press forward in pursuit of it.

I arrived to the first day of summer camp in halfway decent shape and moderate strength, given the one-and-a-half-year hiatus I'd taken from the game. After registration, I drove around to the fieldhouse, past the baseball stadium where the baseball team was already in pre-season form having just come off a national championship that spring. I almost thought about trying out for a spot at third base instead, where I'd avoid the brutal deterioration of my body and likely have a higher probability of a winning record. Our football team was in a rebuild phase, but the baseball and softball teams were expected to steamroll through their schedules with minimal competition.

I grew up modeling my baseball game after Ken Griffey Jr. Whenever the signal permitted, I'd tune into the Mariners' games on my grandpa's old color TV and watch in awe as he succeeded his father in making historic contributions to the greatest game ever played. All of the kids from Daufuskie Island would gather around with their big wood sticks and rubber band balls (our makeshift big-league gear), acting out each at-bat as we dreamed of one day playing in the Majors. I was one of the few lucky enough to play real baseball over in the next county. Some days on the diamond, I thought I was so cool; I swore I was the "Kid" himself. I'd turn my cap backwards and twirl the bat with finesse as I stared the pitcher down, daring him to throw his best heater or slyest curve so I could send it for a ride.

It just so happens that Griffey's number was worn by my grandfather as well, and I followed in my grandfather's footsteps with my desire to play ball as a break from the demands of everyday life. For the love of the game, I could not put the bat down until it no longer felt comfortable in my hands. My grandfather, my father's father, was a stone-cold killer who could play anywhere in the infield and had a big bat the size of a lumberjack. His baseball IQ was out of this world, and he would have played in the Negro leagues had it not disbanded so soon after he entered his prime. In his early days, my grandfather had already shared the field with some of baseball's greatest in

Turkey Stearnes and Joe "Bullet" Rogan (Kansas City Monarchs), James "Cool Papa" Bell (Pittsburgh Crawfords), Martín Dihigo (New York Cubans), James "Red" Moore (Atlanta Black Crackers). and the infamous Josh Gibson, Satchell Paige, Jud "Boojum" Wilson and Smokey Joe Williams (Homestead Grays). There was such a rich history of talent there that it should have been no surprise when I pulled up to my HBCU for the first time to see future hall of famers representing on the ball field.

I swelled with pride at the sight of a majority Black baseball team running like a well-oiled machine, chopping down everything in the path of another baseball title for the university. I snapped back to reality as my cousin's voice rang out across the parking lot. "Yurrrrr! What's good, kuz?!" Even over the shouting from other players excited about the first practice of the season, his voice boomed with distinction. I grabbed my cleats from the backseat and trotted to the locker room, hurriedly dressing out so I wouldn't be the last to hit the field.

The shrill blow of a whistle rang out across the stadium, bouncing off the turf and echoing against the bleachers. The hot sun beamed down on the surface and created a warming effect, baking us as we ran through drill after drill under the watchful eye of our coaches. Head coach K. Phillips shouted at me from the sidelines. "Hicks! What the hell are you doing, son?! Get low, square your base and drive UP; don't let your man have a lower center of gravity than you or he's gonna have a field day." He came closer and put his hand on my shoulder to offer some encouragement. "You've gotta learn your craft. You don't have to be the best nor the fastest, but you have to know how to work the field." It was solid advice that I'd later apply to other aspects of my life.

Coach Phillips was a legend, having won championships at several Division I and II programs before coming back to FACU (where he once played) to retire. Year twenty-five as a head coach and he still hadn't lost his touch. His ability to whip players into shape and teach even the dullest minds how to maneuver the football field like trained soldiers was admirable as far as coaching instincts go, but his ability to fundraise and effectively manage public relations were even more appreciated by the administration. He was nearly as powerful as the Chancellor at FACU, and he certainly spoke with the authoritative demand to support any such suspicion.

FACU offered a chance for me to start fresh with a new identity other than the one I'd created at SSU. There, I was a rockstar, and that legend had followed me here, but I was determined to do things differently this time. I even told people I was from up North, hoping to shake the stigma of my experience growing up in the impoverished lower region of South Carolina.

I started the first few weeks off strong, committing myself to workouts and the adjustment to a higher level of play than I'd been accustomed to. I hit the cafeteria with the team, I woke up for 6:00 am workouts during the week, and I kept my energy up through two and three-a-days, even though some days it felt like I wouldn't make it out of those practices alive. I hit the dummies hard, I shot through my gaps and blew up plays like an All-American in the making. Then another screw came loose, and I lost all of my composure.

My baby brother Israel was a miracle baby. He was born premature after a long, troublesome labor that threatened both his life and that of my mother's. He came into the world fighting, and his infectious spirit warmed the hearts of anyone who came into contact with him. Born under five pounds, the odds of his survival were slim, and when he finally came home, we felt his aura engulf the room as a testament to his divine purpose. Israel was sent especially for my mother, to teach her a love and lesson that would prepare her for heights she'd never imagined.

I fell in love with him as if he were my own son, and I melted whenever he wrapped his little arms around my neck to tell me he loved me. I knew that he would be better than his older brothers, and his light would lead movements of positivity throughout the world wherever he walked. I never thought about a world without my younger brothers in it, because as the oldest, I fully expected them to live a life of longevity far into their old ages. Israel's bubbly personality and cute face was as charming as it gets, and not only did he have me wrapped around his finger, all of my girlfriends who met him loved me even more afterwards. Israel was the sweetest child you could ask for. He was easygoing, soft spoken, and a joy to be around. He was just coming into his own as a preschooler at his new school when tragedy struck.

My brother drowned at his aftercare program while doing a bobbing activity for Halloween. Though the preschool denied any foul play, I knew that there had to be some type of negligence on the school's behalf to allow an activity like this without adequate safeguards or supervision for young children. At the time, my family was knee deep in debt and couldn't afford a retainer for any lawyer, let alone a good one. We struggled through denial after denial and stifled our curses despite one inconclusive explanation after the next, and we wept in between.

I could not bear to see my mother broken this way. My family was falling apart, and I couldn't help but feel helpless as I stood paralyzed by fear and misery. My brother had been a sanctuary for my vulnerability and a stoic who'd restored my faith. His suffering was silent, yet he constantly showed his strength against the strongest deterrents. If only my will was as strong, my purpose as defined as his. His life gave me hope, and his death magnified a world of hurt. I drew parallels from his life to my own in this moment. What began with such promise, and here and now, what was destined to be something so great, had been cut down right before my eyes.

My despondence kept me from practice. I couldn't eat. I couldn't make it out of bed. I stopped communicating with those close to me, and started engaging in wild, promiscuous sex with reckless disregard for my health and safety. I went on a binge with heavy drug use and dangerous acts that placed me in close proximity to peril. I temporarily gave up on life when it seemed clear that I had little left to live for. Of course, I was clouded by the catastrophe that had turned my world upside down in one of the most critical periods of my life. I had taken the faithful leap across the horizon into a new sphere, hopeful for a new beginning, only to find to my surmise that the grass isn't greener on the other side. Another failed experiment. Another muffed curveball of life. I was overwhelmed by loss, and I was on my second strike, desperate not to be counted out.

Death

The pain of a thousand knives slicing through the heart
    of your very being,
The empty feeling inside like an animal gutted alive and
    hung to drip dry,
Flesh rotting, festering in its misery,
The walking dead have no voice with which to protest
    the horrors of a reality beyond imagination,
The insufferable weep hideously but their cries are
    limited to the confines of their own dimensions,
Vividly recanting memories cut short by an unforeseen
    tragedy,
An affair ended by fate Himself,
Oh, Death...indulge me in your wicked ways so that I
    might once again glimpse that face,
And the cursed days spent wishing you were here shall
    be no more,
To turn back the hands of time would be a mercy
    so sweet my lips would lie locked with ineffable
    gratitude,
But alas...the way of the world dictates a life that is
    undeniably transient, and such it is—
May you rest eternally in favor and leisure,
As I await your next kiss.

Lillie Lane

Chapter Eleven

When the calls started coming through, I barely had time to breathe before the phone rang again. One friend, then another, and another. This was the fourth one in the past six months. Death repeatedly hit me like a freight train as old classmates and childhood friends departed from the one place we thought we'd always see each other again. Home was becoming a place where the hopes and dreams of the less fortunate were held hostage until they were halted entirely – by sudden disease or gun violence. When the news of Hilda's tragic ending reached me, I collapsed in confusion. Who? Why? It was nothing to hear about another incident of injustice or unrest denoting the perpetual plight of Palmetto, but this one rocked me to my core. I hadn't even known of her return to the area after so long. While I had managed to find a way out, I had left behind so many people I loved and who loved me, many who I'd never see again. Perhaps it was that familiar feeling of guilt that sent me spiraling. Self-destruction became a form of penance that I accepted because of where I came from, what I had done, and a lifetime of memories that I preferred to leave in the past.

My drug habits had caught up with me once again. This time, the NCAA, and not the school, suspended me for an entire season for not complying with the zero-tolerance policy for a second time. I had no choice but to pick myself up from rock bottom yet again and force myself forward in spite of everything weighing me down. My brother's death suffocated me. The feelings of grief clamped tight down on me like a constrictor of sorts. I didn't know what else to do but let go, let my mind wander until it stopped in a place that no longer hurt to think about.

The replays in my mind of my final moments with some of my most cherished loved ones were a constant reminder of my own inadequacy. As happy as it made me to know they'd reunited beyond Heaven's gates, that acknowledgment kept me in a prolonged state of sadness. At one point, it was all I could do to keep from breaking down. But right here, in this very moment, I was lost in memories.

My mind drifted back to a place of peace, albeit briefly… staring up at the clear sky, I had visions of the haint blue door leading into my grandmother's house as Israel was carried in for the first time, nursing at the sugar-tit, his face mesmerized by the blue bottle tree in the yard that served as a protector from the evil spirits that my ancestors had always warned us about. I felt his little arms hug my neck as his raspy voice entered my ear. I saw his smile and the way my mother would beam down at him, grateful for the gift of her miracle baby. The hairs stood up on my neck; boy, did I miss him so.

I dropped down into a knee bone ring shout, calling out to Yahweh and beseeching him/her for meaning in this tragedy. Mercy had forsaken me, and the clouds grew ominous as the realization set in that life would never be the same for my family. Depression immediately fell upon me, crippling in its quiet rage and torturous wrath. I needed someone. A friend. Surprisingly, that someone would be waiting for me in the chow halls near the Bronco Grill one cold, rainy day.

One of the things I loved most about studying at HBCUs was the diversity of Blackness. Part of what made campuses like FACU feel like home was the abundance of Black and brown prosperity that is celebrated. It's refreshing to see so many who look like me striving towards positive contributions in every sector of society. It's great not being the only or in the minority or having to negate stereotypes or ignore microaggressions as part of your learning environment. The struggle and resilience of our ancestors is felt every day that we walk these campuses; the pride of their persistence is embraced when we walk these halls and look up at the walls; the support of their shoulders is acknowledged when we reach those heights we dream of upon graduation. Their passion for educational liberation and their love for rich legacy lingers on in the hearts of spirited scholars like Lola Lyons, one of the many beautiful people I met along my journey.

She was Eritrean. I called her my Habesha from Heaven. She arrived in my life at a time when I was reserved and afraid of opening back up for fear of losing someone else. She slowly coaxed me out of my shell and allowed her sunshine to pour into my darkness, unlocking the dungeon where I'd placed my heart. Our interactions were poetic. I remember the first time we made love. Her body was a canvas, and when we collided, we created an art so pure and perfect that I sometimes felt the world needed to see. She had a simple, elegant fashion sense that drew the eyes of everyone around her, fueling her aspirations to become a world-famous couturier.

I spent time with Lola as much as I could (even more than I should really), getting lost in our time together and neglecting other, more pressing priorities. She kept my nose wide open. I remember spending Saturday afternoons in the park, serenading her with soliloquies that revealed my sensitivity in the sweetest ways. She knew I was an avid outdoorsman and thought that this was where I preferred to share the depths of my being with her, but really it was my fiscal irresponsibility and relative frugality that led me here. Southern values dictated strict rules about courting, and while I wanted to be intentional in my pursuit, I needed to be conservative in my wooing tactics.

Picnics were cheap, yet intimate. As I'd stare into her honey brown eyes, she reminded me of southern nights sitting under the starry lights of summer skies. Her laughs would effloresce into a contagious euphoria that made it impossible to be upset around her. There was something about her essence.. she just knew what to do and how to move through the spaces of time so effortlessly. Her presence, like Jojo's previously, offered solace in a season of grievance and loss. Beyond just her being there, her love for jazz made me adore her even more. She had a thing for horns, and she could blow too! Her chops on the trumpet put me in a trance, watching her lips softly fill the mouthpiece with hot air that produced notes sweet enough for a lullaby. Melancholy and methodical, her musical style was enchanting in its simplistic selections.

When her mother passed, it brought us even closer together. The news came late one night as we sat eating ice cream on the benches near the Greek plots, mesmerized by the lights above. The moon sat low in the sky, almost at eye level it seemed. It was fat and radiant, like it was on display. I'll never forget that moment. I remember holding her tighter than we've ever held each other, feeling the pain of sadness as if it were my own. There are few things sadder than watching a heart breaking before you, listening as the sounds of grief give way to heaving sobs and streams of tears. Her mother was all she had. I tried my best to maintain my composure as she broke down in my arms, and I knew life would never be the same for either of us. We filled the void of loss with each other's love, until she could no longer bear to be away from home and returned to stay with her father in the comfort of her mother's old room.

The culmination of my freefall towards self-immolation came a few weeks later. Tragedy struck again as I traveled the highway late one night, letting my mind roam as I tried to reassure myself that everything would be okay. In the moment, nothing was, and I became lost in thought wondering if I would ever overcome this chip on my shoulder. After early morning weightlifting and a rough practice, I'd popped a few pain pills to ease the throbbing from my head and shoulder, and as the drowsiness started to set in, I dozed off. Something in my mind startled me awake in the nick of time, a split second before I went over a bridge and headfirst into a ravine below. My eyes got big when I saw my car approaching the short barrier between the road and the big rocks below and I immediately jerked the wheel, veering sharply to the left and clipping a mile marker sign before crossing the three-lane highway and spinning out into the grass and median on the opposite side.

My head was bruised and bloody, my arm stuck at an angle that signaled a sure break. I laid there lifeless for what seemed an eternity, before a good Samaritan stopped to help me. The old man pulled up in his pickup truck, Confederate flag proudly emblazoned on the bumper. He had been coming through Sanford for years but never taken the highway, only back roads. Something (he didn't say what) had told him to jump on the highway that night, and I was humbled by his dutifulness in heeding the call. He took a look and asked if I was okay, then proceeded to dial a wrecker to take care of my vehicle. He let me know that his buddy Jim owned the best tow company around and that it'd be in good hands with him. As I hopped into the truck with the old man, I asked his name and gave him mine. They called him Sen, Creole for "Saint," and I laughed at the irony of it all before leaning my head against the cool window and resting my eyes. What a day.

It was nothing but grace that kept me alive. Still, a part of me died in that crash. I was grateful for it, too, because continuing at the rate I was going would have put me on my death bed before I could accomplish any of the goals I'd set out to achieve years ago. It took me a few weeks to recover after a short stint in the nearby Cone Hospital, but I was blessed to be walking away from this incident under my own power and with everything intact.

It was in that moment that I felt a paradigm shift. I regarded that accident as the impetus for my inception. Those few moments – and in them, the minute details that are oft forgotten in times of tragedy – catalyzed a transformation as I sought out the practice of medicine in my sojourn of self-healing. The ultimate act of liberation, to me, was giving people the power of life, not the illusion of it in financial security. The apprehension of the magnitude of this important mark in my existence would set off the fight of my life. It consummated my raison d'etre. I knew I had to make a stand for something bigger than self, and that was the towering hill upon which I would either prosper or perish.

Kind of Blue provided the soundtrack for that following summer, pacing my stamina as I exercised my stressors away, running miles to the sound of Myles blaring in my eardrum. Ever since I was young, Nana would say, "Mus tek cyear a de root fuh heal de tree." It was just another one of those things I didn't understand back then, but I'd go on to apply it at the core of my medical philosophy. If I was going to shake back, I needed to pull my head out of my ass and act accordingly. This was my designated "summer of strength;" I was hell-bent on reclaiming my life and everything that's mine.

The Pit

"Is anyone up there?"
"Can anybody hear me?"
A voice echoes off the walls of this hole I'm stuck in,
Suicidal thoughts run through my mind leaving me to
    wonder—am I the first? Or one of many men,
Darkness surrounds me, I'm counting my time and only
    it can tell
If I'll ever escape the bonds of this blighted hell...
I feel around me for walls, steps, anything to climb up,
But I'm too late, the Jigsaw has once again declared my
    time up,
So again I fall down into the pit where I began,
Blind to the world, a hopeless fraction of a man,
No night vision to aid me, just intangible dreams,
I'm stuck here for eternity with no way out it seems,
I scream...Free me from these chains that constrict my
    brain,
Free me from this invisible captivity, pity me—
Take mercy on this poor wretched soul,
Rebuild this destruction so that I may once again be
    whole,
Optimism flows heavy in my veins as my feet grow
    weary and so I sit;
To ponder, and await a way out of this pit.

Chapter Twelve

There are so many mistakes you can make that can cost you your life on any given day. Unlike most of my peers, I understood early on that one of the keys to finessing the streets was that the dirt you do out there should never make it back to your front door…but if you stayed in the streets long enough, it always would. The inevitable is inescapable. That mentality saved me; its knell rang loudly throughout my head with every risky decision.

So, I gave up the tough guy persona. I can still fight. I can shoot. But even more, I can annihilate you with my intellect. Intelligence isn't a privilege, it's a gift to be used for the betterment of humanity. The 'Mahatma Gandhis' of the world had found this simple yet effective solution long ago, to the dismay of others. That words and compassion and not violence can rule the world remains as ridiculous a notion as flying pigs, but one day both of those shall come into existence. My fascination ran wild. Whatever my mind could conceive that seemed plausible, I sought strategies for manifestation. The revolution would not and could not be solitary, therefore, my quest to find common ground with men of starkly different beliefs was somewhat obligatory. So, I took a page from brother Martin's book and sought relatability to my cause.

I thought about one of the first courses I'd taken at SSU, entitled "Dissecting the Diaspora." One of the more poignant yet empowering realizations of the HBCU experience is how much of our history is discredited in world history. Across the globe, the plight of Black people has routinely set the stage for tomorrow's promise. It's impossible to isolate any period in time without acknowledging the contributions and influences of melanated populations. The course examined the effects of Christianity and the Baptist church on Black spirituality and healing practices, as well as the intersection of music, religion and sports with the Black identity and capacity. We cannot allow ourselves to be coddled by feelings of inadequacy and longing for a heavenly home in lieu of manifesting the reality we want here on Earth. The persisting belief that we are merely entertainers rather than creators and innovators and thinkers diminishes our value to society. Ownership is key. It's why countless young boys like myself set out to kill, steal and destroy...not simply for the sake of thinly veiled power vacuums and world domination like our melanin-deficient counterparts, but rather for a feeling of pride in having something. Because money seemed to birth opportunity, it was the object of both our obsession and ostension. I reflected on youthful misdeeds driven by a desperation for money. I recounted the instances of deranged aggression sparked by the tension that exists between men born from similar cultural and ethnic backgrounds and the manner in which those brothers are pitted against each other for survival. "Eureka!" My mind exploded once more with the passion of conviction. Medicine, one of the true sustainable demands of the world, was a pursuit that I knew would garner the income that I would need to make my dreams come true. A life-changing, multi-generational blessing awaited me in this career. In that moment it became so much more than that though. More than a sum of the audacity of my ambition, medicine would provide a catapult into global impact, social liberation, and reclamation of identity...a means by which to revolutionize the matrix which had been forced upon our existence.

My greatest regret is my underestimation of what it means to be young, gifted, and Black, and the power I behold as a result. I blew opportunities and left hands unshaken out of ego and misguidance. It became my purpose to help reverse the course of youth who, like myself, became equally misguided in their ambitions and emotions because of the issues that plague their existence. I wanted to help fulfill the dreams of those who would fall victim to defeatist mentalities and squander potential out of feelings of hopelessness.

The government-sanctioned exploitation of education created a cancerous spread of misinformation and financial despair among much of the middle and working class. I was thankful for an introduction to the pitfalls of these predatory practices by private lenders, and I acknowledged the intentional inequity of an otherwise well-intentioned philosophy behind the government's push for a more educated citizenry.

As my perspective grew, I came to understand the fine line between education and intelligence. I recognized the distinctions; how being educated grants access, whereas being intelligent grants ascens on. Knowing is the separation factor for many people, the difference between words that produce wisdom and understanding and those that simply pander to social puppets who regurgitate what they are told.

I also learned to value second-hand knowledge. Learning vicariously from and through the experiences of credible, reputable sources with real skin in the game has helped me establish familiarity with situations to better navigate or even circumvent them when placed in my path. Knowledge and wisdom aren't the same. Oftentimes the nuanced discernment that distinguishes these two comes from vicarious ascertainment of information.

As a minor example, watching those around me lose their lives in one way or another while being active in the streets sent a clear message of inevitability. There were usually only two places you'd end up when living that lifestyle. What scared me so much about my criminal behavior was that I was so good at it. I was good at doing dirt and getting off scot-free. I knew that the longer my lucky streak, and the better I became at finessing crime, the bigger the target would become on my back until it'd be impossible to escape. As with anything, the better you are at your craft, the bigger the threat posed. When those repercussions could mean losing your life to death or incarceration, it's time to reconsider the arena you want to be playing and succeeding in.

Growth elevated my mind to higher ground, transforming my thought process and infusing grace into the formula from which I derived my decisions in specific situations. Rather than wield my intellect as a sword of supremacy, I learned to employ it as an olive branch of reconciliation. It was time to ascend. The only thing standing in the way of my dreams was me. It was time to finish what I started when I set out on this paper chase several years prior, and I was determined to honor that commitment with the appropriate displays of action.

For me, college was no longer a sprint but a marathon to be endured, a test of will and perseverance rather than pure acceleration and drive. I was headed back to my true home, returning to the campus where it all began and where my passion was first sparked. It was time to get back to business. I was putting athletics behind me and turning the page on a devastating chapter of my life that I'd held onto for far too long. With my brother in my heart and my eyes on the prize, I was SSU-bound. I could do this. I *had* to do this.

Red Robin

Sitting there, painting the branch upon which it sits
with its brilliant red hue,

With its breast inflated and feet perched it glares off in
the distance, eyes red too,

Unlike most birds, however, this one says nothing;
no chirps nor cheery singing, silence haunts the
surrounding air,

Its dazzling crimson feathers bleed with despair,

Head cocked like a trigger, body poised like a statue,
nothing seems wrong to the average eye,

Yet, inside, it cringes with the pain of a million knives, its
red beauty never again to stain the sky,

Tears flow like red rivers down its coat, like a red shirt
that bleeds when washed, it grieves,

Its cries start to ring out across an empty forest in search
of something or someone, bursting the eardrums
of happiness and deafening the world with its
desperation,

Nothing else exists in these moments; left in the world
all alone

To mourn expired successes and fend for its own,

An injured wing leaves it handicapped with the thought
that all hope is lost; it'd be better off dead,

Pessimism drowns its mind and prevents it from
flapping ahead,

Dread not defeat—when we fall, we must pick ourselves
back up;

Success is not given to those who stay down.

The road to triumph isn't easy; you may get hurt,

The harrowing grip of misery shall offer testament to
   your work, a test of your will to survive...
If only this robin knew that with a little bit of faith and
   hard work it could once again fly,
And its radiant red glory could once again paint the sky.

Chapter Thirteen

I was hungry for a rebirth to propel me forward in my new walk, equipping myself with spiritual tools to complement the wisdom of experience that I now took with me on this journey. I started attending a contemporary church near campus that catered to millennial worshippers, an attempt to repackage the Gospel of old. One Sunday after service, an old lady who reminded me of one of the church mothers from Cool Spring Baptist back home stopped me and told me she saw the light on me. I could barely see her face beneath the big hat that matched the vibrant colors of her pantsuit, but I could hear the power and authority with which she spoke. I didn't truly know what she meant, but I thanked her and went on with my day.

Later that night, my mind was racing as I sat and tried to figure out what it was about this light that I couldn't see or feel. I thought back to the time when I was a young boy, protected by my innocence. I racked my brain trying to remember who I was before the world got to me, before the powers that be told me who I should be. When I left the comfort of home to venture out into the world, I felt the pressure to conform to society's expectations in order to meet the demands which accompanied my goals. I kept my image "clean and collected" to avoid stereotypes when attempting to navigate professional spaces or diminish any appearance of a threat when interacting with law enforcement. I never severed ties with the set, but I changed how I moved. I pulled up on the block many days straight from the office—work badge tucked tightly away in the jacket pocket of my tailored suit—as if my presence somehow offered validity to the idea of being Black at home congregating in a suspicious area where suspicious activity is rampant, minding our own damn business.

I always knew it shouldn't matter, until one day came with a crushing confirmation that it doesn't—and not in a positive way. Wearing a suit didn't make me a superhero. Neither bespoke dress nor proper speech, professional mannerisms, nor a well-kempt appearance could save me from persecution, no matter how polished I was.

The realities of my experiences and of those around me compelled me to come from the shadows and cast a light, illuminating the lessons learned throughout. The most important realization was that I didn't have to wait to become "somebody" before people would take me seriously. If you speak loudly enough, boldly enough, emotionally and intelligibly enough, people will listen. Even if you don't do any of those things, there's still an audience for you; "your gift will make room for you," as they say. We can be whoever we aspire to be—but the journey will require monumental tasks for some, in comparison to most, that will make the dream seem impossible. We must think beyond.

I'd always played life more on the defense, flowing with the tide rather than shifting sails and taking hold of the opportunities that arose before me. It was a tad too much consideration that stalled my takeoff from those tethered days of yesterday. Once the realization came, it offered a rare gift to relate to certain lifestyles without being entrenched in them.

Every strong defensive personality has a natural counterattack that is lethal in its swift surprise. Like the wing-back that swipes a ball near the eighteen and takes it up the sideline instead of playing the safe long ball ahead, or the linebacker that intercepts a slant and finds a seam to take it to the house instead of hitting the turf, when a wolf sees an opportunity to strike it attacks almost instinctively.

As my approach to conflict evolved, so did my tactics. My techniques, though much more reserved, became sharper in their deployment. The killer instinct must constantly be refined in preparation for the unfamiliar foe. Diplomacy is always my default, but I let it be known that violence is never not on the table.

It was the transition to the Cobra Kai mantra of "strike first, strike hard, no mercy" that put me in an offensive mind frame where I imposed my will unapologetically in expression of my talents, though I maintained a sense of humility that tried not to exercise my dominance to the detriment of my peers. It was the discernment of when to lay on the gas and when to take a more reserved approach that I developed through my experiences. This framework was tied, in part, to a mantra developed from the gang mentality I grew up with.

It was a funny thing, the way society's sadistic ways often set in motion the unfortunate circumstances that we take for granted. In a country where, for quite some time, the laws of the land regarded certain men as inferior solely based on complexion or race or geographic origin, it is hard not to see how crime evolved parallel to that political process. As such, the crime-ridden communities that minorities were systematically subjected to – whether through redlining practices or forced migrational patterns (Southern violence, natural disasters, economic/political inequity, etc.) – became a naturally recurring repercussion of the racial bias that America was built upon. In a state of deprivation and despair, who better to prey on for your wants and needs but a man who has little or no rights? It is but the most basic and natural survival instinct to seek what we lack along the path of least resistance.

Over time, though now "free" of the laws that kept us locked in chains or languishing under Jim Crow rule, our community has imploded because through the lens of the law, it is easier to rob, kill or steal from a Black man than practically anyone else in America. For that reason – at least in part – I was intentional about my demographic discretion in identifying targets for my devilish acts.

Deep in the mountains of western Kentucky, in a small football town is where I committed my first robbery. One of the nation's largest and most prestigious research universities sat squarely in the valley, geographically isolated from the world outside of Blackstone. I would hang with my cousins over the summers in high school, and we would wreak havoc in the neighborhoods of unsuspecting, privileged college students whose possessions were meal tickets for kids like us. What our parents saved months and even years for, these kids would dispose of at the slightest inconvenience or leave unsecured in unlocked vehicles without regard. Back on Daufuskie, we didn't have the luxuries of technology. I got my hands on enough devices up here in Blackstone to feed a few families for months in the Lowcountry. I would repurpose the devices to students of more modest means, if you could even phrase it as such, and I started a college fund for my siblings so we could each start school with at least $1,000 in expenses saved up.

One evening, I was showing off and wanted to flex my muscles against an Asian man walking home to his apartment near campus. I recognized him from a party we were at weeks earlier, and I remembered him being drunk enough to hurl racial slurs at the "little monkeys" who'd somehow received an invitation to a college party. We were underage and not looking for trouble, so we brushed it off in the moment. Now, on this dimly lit street where he was outnumbered by these "little monkeys," I saw my opportunity to teach him a lesson. See, for generations Asians and other immigrant groups came to the United States and bypassed the second-class citizen treatment bestowed upon Black Americans. In turn, they turned their noses up and espoused some of the same discriminatory ideals they'd fought against and even fled their native homes for. Instead of co-existing as individuals bonded by shared struggles of oppression, the targets on our backs grew bigger.

I approached the man under the streetlight and asked him if he had any money to spare for a few hungry monkeys. I saw him pause and clutch his iPhone and briefcase closer, then watched as his eyes grew wide with terror upon recognition of our faces. I could tell he never expected to see us again or have to answer for his bigoted speech. When he refused, I threatened to take everything in his possession. "All I want is your iPhone, but if you don't give it up, I may end up taking your life instead."

Of course, I knew I would never hurt someone over materials, let alone kill them. But I wanted him to know I meant business. He started backpedaling, and as I walked closer toward him, I drew my pocketknife for a more convincing display of aggression. He pleaded and begged for mercy, while I laughed hysterically at how quickly the tables can be turned. My brother tugged at my arm, begging me to leave him alone. "It's not worth it, Kam, just let him go," my brother exclaimed. The honor he had in standing up for this man who likely wouldn't do the same if he were in a position of peril was commendable. It froze me in my tracks and made me swell with pride inside. I knew then that my brother's heart was pure and not yet tainted by the realities of a world that showed no love to people like us. We walked away, leaving the man with his possessions and what little dignity he had left in that moment. An eye for an eye was no way to live. Without knowing it, my brother had saved my life that night. Decades later, it tormented me to no end that I couldn't do the same for him.

It was the lessons from these pivotal life moments that prepared me for the challenge of pledging a fraternity. I'd come from two generations of honorable, high-achieving Greek men who'd forged their own paths to and through the toil of pledging. When it came time for me to show interest by attending a smoker, I dressed to the nines in my sharpest suit, tie, and Allen Edmonds dress shoes. They were hand-me-downs, but I wore them with pride and a flair that was oh so debonair.

I kept my head down and didn't draw too much attention, because when it came time to get down, I already knew I'd have a lot of heat coming my way. Word had spread through the circles of Nu Kappa Alpha that I was attempting to associate myself with their SSU chapter, and I prepared myself for the consequences that came along with that desire. Unknowingly, my entire life to date prepared me for the privilege of joining this noble clan of brothers who aspired to excellence in every field of human endeavor. Over the next few months, I would endure the ultimate test of time and will.

At the end of our first week as pledges, we received our commissary of nickels, licorice, and condoms. We wore a dog collar around our necks and vowed to wear the same black t-shirt and black jeans for the remainder of our process. We had no idea how long or what was in store, we just knew it was about to get hot and hazy with no signs of letting up anytime soon. My Dean and Associate Dean of Pledges were both locked in for this one, and as eager as they were to return our chapter to greatness after a twenty-year hiatus, we were sure it was about to be a wild ride.

Some few months later, Hell Night finally rolled around. It was our last trial before being welcomed into the bond. It was one for the books, a night that would be forever ingrained in the depths of my mind. An opportunity to revisit the pains of knowing things just weren't exactly right, but that they'd never be the same. Our line name was the "Advocatus," a testament to our proclivity for altruistic endeavors. I was the Rokk, responsible for holding the line down through any adversity we might face along the way. Enduring 133 days, 4 hours, and 12 minutes of hell made me consider a career in the Marine Corps. I was more disciplined than I'd ever been.

Marching into a shadowy dungeon in the cellar of an old corn mill, I tapped my front and back to make sure they were ready for whatever would go down in this room. We gripped up as a mob of masked men entered silently, dressed in black and unidentifiable by gait or demeanor. The moon beamed down on us through the glass ceiling above, and the brilliance of that rutilant diamond shining brightly in the night sky as my head stayed stuck in "scope" was eternally etched into my temporal lobe.

"Greetings, big brothers, how do you do this day? As for me, I can't complain, it's just my normal cry for Phi…" Our voices were drowned out by loud sirens in the distance. We had no idea what was going on as the sounds grew closer, but we did know that none of us were going to stick around to find out. After just two hours, it was time to cut the fun short.

Alas, I had crossed those fiery sands and become a "Nu" man. I was battle-tested and ready to conquer the world. Back on campus, we marched to the plot, tired and sweaty, awaiting the crowds that had gathered to see our arrival. I spotted my ex-girlfriend off in the distance, eyes tracking her as she made her way to me to congratulate me on my newfound success. I quickly flashed back to our relationship, a fiery back-and-forth exchange of power and pleasure that fueled the passion we shared between each other. We shared a hometown and homeroom classroom in secondary and we were competitive to a fault with each other. Especially her. She'd grown up with four brothers and always had to fight for what she wanted. We went at it over school subjects, sports, even politics. The two of us made routine bets on things like what was more likely to happen first: witnessing the first impeachment of a Supreme Court justice or going to war with China. There was always money involved too, and I rarely won. She'd kicked my ass at every level of life through college.

As she walked up, we embraced briefly and exchanged small talk until my eyes began to undress her in that familiar way she knew all too well. She blushed and walked away, reminding me how I never kept my promise to write her a poem.

The truth is, I had written that poem a thousand times in my mind. I drifted off into a daydream of days past. I remembered her from our earlier college days, cautious and well-collected. I saw her face the last time we'd spoken, right in the midst of one of my major meltdowns. Our break was far from clean, ugly in fact. I failed a major exam exactly one week later, a class we took together. I recall sitting there, dejected, knowing that she reveled in my pain as payback for what had happened between us. Her face twisted with pleasure, totally engulfed with epicaricacy over my situation. Maybe it was the way I'd yelled at her in my frustration when all she wanted to do was plan a date to the opera. Yet another bond broken and missed opportunity I guess.

Now was different though. The vibe seemed fresh and rather invigorating. We still had so much in common. Her ambition was even more awe-inspiring. She was a finance major on her way to becoming a corporate analyst, maybe even a Wall Street banker. We shared a Greek letter, her sorority founded just a few years before mine. I couldn't let this interaction pass without putting one final touch on our 10-year tenure.

You asked me to write a letter, and I couldn't think of any one better...than K. Beyond a name, K is the energy of kindred spirits—a symbol of rainbows that came after the rain...a beautiful construct resting at the base of all that is kind, and considerate of the killing fields that lie awaiting Black kids like us who fantasize about kingdoms here on Earth rather than in Heaven...K is a letter crafted particularly with us in mind, intertwining the feelings we bury deep within, uniting us as kin as we consummate the kind of love most only dream of. When they mention my life story, your voice, your presence will be the keynote that kept on giving.

K.....a letter kindling memories of the fiery paths taken towards those burning sands, compelling us to bow on the name of Kappa or carry those ivies as crosses heavy with the burdens we each bear. The experiences we share, worth more than the sum of all the letters in the alphabet, more than any amount of karats in a bracelet, brighter than any diamond, and shinier than any pearl...I love you, girl. Drunk off blended cocktails of lust and loathing, your beauty, kaleidoscopic through the lens of my love, takes me to the heights and depths of my imagination, for better or for worse...my life has been kidnapped by the karma of connection. May your lips speak the words of liberation that unbridle my emotions, may your body be the key that unlocks the kingdom of black magic in which we seek to dwell into eternity...

Yours Sincerely,
Kam

I dropped the note in the mail, addressing it to the one place I knew she'd always return to. Her childhood home, on a dirt road just a few miles from the one I grew up on, was her healing place. It was her haven when she needed space to regroup, to escape the hustle and bustle of life on the incessant hamster wheel. I wanted to leave her with a final goodbye, a flurry of feelings jumbled into words that would offer a closing departure that was years overdue.

Soon I would be trapped in a foreign world, confined to my own mind and riddled with emotional exhaustion as I committed myself completely to the crucible of medical school.

It took me two years to get my mind right after pledging. I almost died and I didn't let any of my line brothers know. In fact, while they gathered at fall graduation to celebrate the memories of our Hell Night, I was confined to a dark, lonely hospital ward, wishing for a way out. From that day forward, I grew distant from the demands of fraternity life. It wasn't that the process took too much out of me; it was that I put too much in, which left me with too many questions.

I grew up in an environment where loyalty meant everything, and the boys you got it in blood with became brothers who you'd do anything for. Accordingly, I went above and beyond to look out for my LBs in every way possible. I sacrificed my pockets and my priorities. There was nothing I wouldn't do for any one of them. Early on in our process, however, I suspected there was a leak on our line, and I was determined to get to the bottom of it. Sometimes, to find a rat you have to set a trap, and so that's what I did.

I gave false but innocent information about some girls I was hanging with to see who'd run back and tell them what I said. These girls had done the same to a friend of mine, so an eye for an eye provided some justification in light of the situation. It was an unfortunate sacrifice, but it was necessary at the time to get the confirmation I sought. There are casualty principles in business and war that maybe these men would understand one day if they were to aspire to the heights envisioned in their minds. Sure enough, one of my LBs ran back and spilled the "news" I'd shared with them in confidence and jest. I later disclosed my false statement, but I knew that I'd never give these men my all again.

On the other hand, I was inspired beyond imagination at what my LBs had accomplished in such a short time span of their lives, and I saw a little of myself in each of them. By their age, I'd already dabbled in so much and achieved so many accomplishments that transcended beyond university campuses or even national borders, but I'd also failed countless times in pursuit of the next big thing. I'd lost people closest to me and nearly lost myself and my mind in the process. I'd been tested against the best and brightest in national talent identification programs and elite private schools, pitted against peers whose family status made mine look like a charity case, and I'd turned down opportunities to further that trajectory at institutions where the pedigree carried with it a presumption of future promise. I betted on myself and forged my own path, and along the way I squandered plenty of potential that made many (including myself) wonder why I hadn't elevated to a higher place by now. Every minute of every day I was consumed with thoughts, emotions, rage...I couldn't shake my past. I had escaped a life of crime to accomplish the impossible, yet looking around at the successes and immense talents of my brothers, I knew that what I was doing wasn't nearly enough.

And so, I went harder. I didn't party, though I wanted to wet the floor with some shoulders that would make poodles purr and pearls clutch. I didn't kick it or pull up to fraternize or fellowship with my normal crew because I was ashamed of who I was. In my mind, I hadn't done enough for the privilege of portraying an image of anything but an aspirant—not someone who'd already made it. Accordingly, I believed that my silence would serve my peers better, allowing them to navigate our post-pledging days without my input in order to minimize the influence of my previous crucibles on this critical life experience for them. My father, throughout my upbringing, implied that every boy should grow into a man on his own. So, it was partly that consideration, along with my own selfishness, that kept me off the scene.

I didn't realize to what extent others needed me... to tell my story, to use my experiences as a light to keep the darkness away from their own lives. I had overcome the odds to get there. Through it all, I remained solid too. I was made right, but I hadn't quite made it in life...and that frustrated me to the point that I obsessed over it. I couldn't even be around other people without getting lost in my own thoughts, and so I stayed away, regretfully. Months became years and years became too late; death took its usual toll, and brothers who I'd missed dearly departed to their new destination without so much as a goodbye. It eats at me still, like a hunger that I can't satisfy no matter how little I crave.

I visited my brother's grave and laid a splendid bouquet of carnations by his head, patting his headstone three times in homage to our journey together. He'd done well and fought hard, and there was peace in that. I tilted my loving cup back, drank heartily, and poured the rest out onto the ground in one final toast. What we all knew within Nu Kappa Alpha was that "friends never part." There was beauty in the belief that unification would happen on the other side of those golden shores. To days of yore good brother, until we meet again.

Listen

Fireflies burn yellow stains in the black of the night sky
as I lay there,
Gazing up at the stars, identifying each one as one of
the gods—
Maybe they don't live there, maybe they just play there,
Whatever the truth is, the paintings at church don't
match the description,
Racking my brain trying to figure out just who this God
is, I hear a voice that says "listen,"
"Open your mind to things unseen, your ears to words
unspoken; allow yourself to dream,
Remember, there is more to life than what it seems,
Pay close attention, hear the angelic voices of the gods
sing,
Oh, indeed, who could imagine a King...!"
Erotic emotions pass over me with the floating breeze,
and yet again I hear nothing, but
"Listen..."
The harmonious trumpets of Heaven play a fanfare that
only the keenest of ears can hear,
May these wise words move you, and to your heart be
kept dear,
"Release your conviction and relax into submission;
The transition is in effect, my child...now listen."

Lillie Lane

Chapter Fourteen

I always knew I'd be a doctor because of what it meant to be one when I saw my father. My pops was known for many things, but aside from his aptitude, the first thing that came to mind for me was his way of speaking in a sharp, breviloquent tongue that was to be regarded as a matter of fact, or else. He always let you know that he meant business in so many words and was rarely challenged by anyone, other than my mother in the short time they spent together.

Pops was constantly pontificating about the immoral thrills of first world mentalities and how the spoils of excess drove hospital admissions rates around the country. Though not often the reported diagnosis, greed sent men to their deathbeds in droves, and my father wasn't at all forgiving of the unnatural desire for the almighty dollar. His stinginess would immunize him from ever slipping into indebtedness. Like all men, my father was flawed—a testament to his humanity. But he was a brilliant doctor, and I studied him laboriously to glean whatever I could from his tactics. He had medical insight far beyond most of the world's top physicians, and he took himself and his calling seriously. I could fill textbooks with the knowledge I gained from him alone. Unlike him, however, I found comfort in classrooms amongst my peers, deciding to forego following in his footsteps and instead pursuing my MD at a historically Black college.

Meharry Medical College was full of masterminds like myself who opted for an educational experience that embodied Black excellence over one that enabled white elitists.

The world is often disillusioned by the appeal of elitism. This is especially true in higher education, where aristocracy rules admissions processes and perpetuates cycles of inequity intertwined with pretentiousness, as if the essence of these institutional admissions processes and their decisions alone aren't elitist enough. There's undeniable enjoyment in exclusivity. Even my father, in his unashamed Blackness and appreciation of the historic iniquities that created the opportunity gaps our medical systems were founded upon, came to prioritize a certain pedagogical pedigree as the stamp of true promise — a meritocracy within an even greater meritocracy, if you will.

My ancestors came over from Angola, partly landing in Virginia in the 1600s and later in northern Colombia, splitting us amongst the Americas. My family in the States would trickle further down below the Mason-Dixon to Carolina—James Island to be exact—and my darker family who'd been deposited closer to the equator made their way southeast from Cartagena de Indias to join the people of San Basilio de Palenque.

The first free African slave town in the Americas, Palenque has a rich history and an iron will that was passed on from the days of Biohó. It was a walled city that stayed mostly isolated from assimilation into the Spanish way of life, maintaining ancestral traditions that live on today. As was necessary both then and still to this day, we as a people thrived in isolation as a protective and preservative measure in furtherance of a future that could avoid the fateful destruction of so many subcultures like ours. My family carried the blood and traditions of our Angolan ancestors, though one side more proudly than the other. While I like to think my overall flavor came from that dazzling beauty and Palenquero style, my flair for conjuring came in the states; there was no denying the mysteries of the medicine magic passed on through the Gullah Geechee practices along our corridor of Carolina.

Original herbalism as practiced in our communities was a different type of medicine that society had since strayed from and could never truly embrace or even understand...one that modern medicine would not allow my father to recognize despite his own deep Angolan roots. Like much of our history, colonizers had distorted our religious and medical practices to force a perspective of barbarism, diminishing our work to witchcraft and Devil worshiping because they couldn't comprehend it. They then forced us to believe those same lies. The truth is far less sinister and more nuanced than the misinformed take it to be.

Pouring through the notes of my great grandfather, a well-known root doctor in the Lowcountry, I realized that there was an innate consciousness in the products of nature that surrounded us, and that by utilizing those natural forces—sometimes in combination with the power of the dead—we could heal and restore in ways unlike those seen in medical rooms. Since it was believed that illness was a manifestation of both natural and supernatural causes, traditional African healers known as Sangomas or Inyangas would serve as mediums to treat patients using both physical and spiritual means, through animal offerings, divination, exorcisms, ritualistic incantations, and minerals and herbs. These practices, like the blended Palenquero language, were based in Bantu origins. This ancestral cosmology was created to effect precise and calculated outcomes of liberation from white hegemonic oppression.

Owing its origins to Benin, where ancestors first channeled the spirits of Sakpata (an earth god, responsible for the cohesion and stability of the individual, and, more importantly, the health and well-being of everything) and Legba and paid homage to the Egungun in order to unlock the gateways to their higher calling, Vodoun (a Creole cultural branch of the more commonly known Voodoo/Vodou religion) was proof that light exists amongst the darkness; you just have to find it. It was principled on, among other things, the belief that you reap what you sow. As you worship your voodoo, so shall it honor you. Like Christianity, it is also rooted in sacrifice, yet the offerings usually take the shape of blood sacrifices instead of tithes and offerings. This art came to be known as Conjure or root work as its perception altered.

As with all our contributions to society, outsiders tried to steal and take credit for the healing they'd witnessed at the hands of root doctors. They incorporated what was actually hoodoo (which lacked any basis in theology) into Western movies and literature, appropriating practices that they didn't truly understand. The only problem was, these outsiders could not manifest the dark matter in the same way. Lest we forget that energy never dies, it is only transferred to a different realm. These outsiders didn't understand alteration of energy, and consequently, turned carbon's atomic properties into a sign of evil, with 6-6-6 marking some great beast, when truly this was the work of skilled alchemists in a form unrecognizable to the outsiders for obvious reasons.

For me, this was a different type of abolitionist work reflecting a craft that I could claim as my own, distinct from the teachings of Western practitioners who'd developed their theories to our detriment. Society had gone to great lengths to demonize our original practices rooted in nature. Their books could not account for the oral history of a craft derived from foreign origins and passed down through generational keepers of its secrets. Its magic took on various forms and demanded vastly different preparation, depending on its intended use. If not a tool for Black healing and salvation it was a mechanism of spiritual warfare, though it wasn't until years later that I intended to use it as such.

I wanted to make a difference in reclaiming Black lives within a field where we were under appreciated. I suppose that had I any real sense of direction and purpose prior to embarking upon my eight-year journey in the study of modern medicine, I would have shortened my journey and gone to law school instead. Saving lives and prescribing just mercy, often in a time when people needed it most, is an eerie reflection of the work advocates do in and out of courtrooms every day. The pervasive nature of "reasonableness" throughout the letter of the law spoke to its dynamic nature, not entirely unlike medicine; reasonable is an ever-changing concept induced as much by subjectivity as it is objectivity.

The law, as society regards it, is an ugly beast—yet we must exalt those who dare dig deep enough to reveal its beauty and bring out its best qualities in order to effect positive change. I view the law in the same manner that I view life, as a science... and science is an experiment, full of opportunities to learn and grow and optimize the conditions around us. This sentiment affirms my love of the land and the duty I find in its stewardship. It led me to my first pair of overalls and to my groundbreaking work in the garden of medicine.

Society had been under medical inducement for far too long. We overprescribed medications instead of treating the entire individual, inclusive of the physical, mental, emotional, and spiritual facets of our beings. Holistic medicine focused on treatment *and* prevention, a component sorely lacking from the practice of Western medicine, which was much more symptom driven. Our ancestors believed in unlocking the innate healing abilities in each of us, relying on natural properties to provide solutions. The constant misdiagnosis and mistreatment of the bodies of Black women in particular had been a cause for alarm for quite some time. The allopathic medicine practiced by Western doctors emphasized a biochemical/biomedical approach that observed microorganisms and diseased cells. The inherent bias in many physicians and their less-than-intimate familiarity with Black women's bodies has led to subpar service delivery and dangerous decisions for patients in the care of these providers.

This was what I had been called to do. I wish my brother had been there alongside me, as we made our mark on medicine together. I remember vividly the events of that day when they took him away, and how I'd cried for days…weeks…months even. I cried until the tears no longer flowed, until there was nothing left but emptiness and headaches and questions about what should have been. I've never felt like such a failure in life until that moment. I had not only let my brother down; indeed, I felt like I had forsaken my entire family. I blamed myself for the string of tragic events that befell our family over the past several years, wondering if somehow my actions had cursed us all and riddled us with bad luck until my demise. I suppose that thought was as much a part of my reason for leaving as my desire to immerse myself in the medicinal practices of the Motherland. As much as I was running towards something, I was running away as well.

Alas, it was time for me to set out on my life's career path and embrace the responsibilities that came along with it. On the day before I left, I secretly took the ferry down to my father's place off the Coosawhatchie River, his mansion towering above the others. My imagination always took me back to the days of olde, when the Coosa Indians (after which it was named) roamed these lands and this river, flowing from it into the river Broad and then out the sound into the Atlantic. If only to see the peaceful wilderness of America before it was colonized and commercialized into its current state, I'd cherish a jaunt into nature's time machine.

My father wasn't home, and I was all the more appreciative for this absence, unlike the others. I was there to send one final message before my departure, before leaving this old life behind.

My entire life to date, I've had a love/hate relationship with my father. He was someone who talked the talk but didn't walk the walk when it came to basic principles of morality and family values. I do believe there are men who are as good as they are bad. Don't get me wrong, my father was absolutely the hero in many people's stories, but he had long since stopped being the hero in mine. I'd once looked up to his shrewd and cold ways because for a time I truly believed that to reach the top you had to be an asshole, and maybe that meant distancing yourself even from those you love in order to do so. I couldn't have been more wrong.

I resented the fact that he never quite saw the errors of his ways and I always held hope that one day he'd wake up and realize that in his quest for success he had often sacrificed one of the greatest gifts one ever receives—family. How naive of me. I'd since given up on the apology that I'd waited year after year for. I loved my father unconditionally, and in my own healing process, I discovered a truth that the world knows all too well— that hurt people, hurt people.

I was frequently reviled by my father. No matter what I did, it was never quite good enough. I realize now that his absence was a necessary burden of his ambitions. My insistence on perfection in an attempt to please him from afar was a product of his incessant drilling of the 12 P's of planning into my head. "Piss poor preparation promotes piss poor performance; piss poor performance promotes pain." I'd dished out my fair share of pain and I wouldn't allow myself to follow those same footsteps again. because I knew I would hate myself for it. I had the power to break generational cycles and I was determined to end this one right here, at his doorstep.

When I arrived, I walked around to the back and slipped through the gate near the boathouse so as not to be seen by any neighbors. I wrote, "Life gives us opportunity upon opportunity to right the wrongs of our past and give back to those who sacrificed so much on our behalf. Eventually, those opportunities cease to arise, the picture comes into focus and shines a bright spotlight on your character flaws, and those sacrificial lambs lose sight of any potential they saw in you for good. Soon, the world will follow suit. Eventually, the incessant rain comes to a stop and the sun shines bright on those dark, damp, ugly spots. Accordingly, the truth about who we are always comes to light. May you—and the rest of the world— hate what you see in your past as much as I do. But today, I choose to love you, like I always have...yet this time without bitterness. I choose to forgive you and thank you for everything you've given me. Without knowing, you've made me a better man than I ever thought I could be. For that, I'm forever grateful to be your son. Take care, Pop."

I folded the note and placed it gently in a bright red envelope, impossible for him to miss when it was time. I affixed the wax seal with the acronym "Φ3," an abbreviated version of our fraternal vow to stay "forever faithful to the frat." I tucked it in the seat of his favorite water cruiser. He'd find it eventually. on one of his early morning rides out to the sound, perhaps. That was one of his favorite pastimes during the spring months. Those were the last words I ever got to say to my father, albeit on parchment and not in person.

I waited until dusk set in then crept off like a thief in the night. I made it to my port an hour away and got settled, preparing to wait out my ship's arrival the next morning with only the overcast sky and the sound of ocean waves swaying and splashing against the bulkhead to keep me company. I reset the clock ticking furiously inside of me, making peace once more with my situation before the pending embarkation.

Lying there in the eigengrau of blanket darkness, I was assaulted by a truth that would open my eyes clearly to who I was and what I'd yet to become. Potential is but a hollow placeholder; a pointless noun bestowing praise upon those who lack the hunger and vigor of their convictions. It's a placid comfort for the hopefuls who've yet to transform their action into capacity. Some of the prime years of my life had been squandered living in the realm of potential, but I knew a change of residency was imminent. First, I just needed to topple the elephant that entered every room with me, occupying unwanted space and deterring those who approached me out of adoration and recognition.

Somewhere along the way I'd lost my light, but I wasn't sure when, where or how it happened to start to reclaim it. It was the reason I carried such a big chip on my shoulder. I had undergone much of this middle phase of my life – between adolescence and adulthood – as an underachiever. I don't mean that in relation to my peers necessarily, but rather in consideration of my squandered potential. It was like a smell that emanated only enough for intimate detection, yet its pungency lingered in the nasal passages as a constant reminder to me and those close to me that I was stinking up the place. To the rest of the world, I walked convincingly in that stench, feigning smiles to hide the shame and repulsive odor of ordinariness.

Illusions

I am not who I appear to be...
It's clear to see that your fear of me is not that I should
    impale you with my intellect,
But rather that I might seize you in a vicious grasp and
    unleash the wrath of a man scorned,
War torn and battle-tested, a diamond thus emerges
    from pressure,
The incarnation of a dream deferred.
Though the luster may fade it must shine again,
As a clock moves the sun rises again,
Erasing the errors of yesterday, winding up for the wins
    of tomorrow,
My soul cries out from depths unknown to most,
Speaking the sweet sentiments of memories past,
Reflecting on the boy who became a man that would
    conquer the world...
If only he could rein in the demon of time,
If only, if only...there was but a wish—
The places he'd gone, the places he'd missed,
Smooth sailing over troubled waters is a compliment to
    the ship,
High and tight captain, you must never lose your grip,
Aye aye great mate,
With a heart of cheer and opportunity looming near,
I dare say that were you to link your destiny with mine,
Two fates intertwined into one mind—
Together we'd truly be one of a kind,
For though I am but a stranger to you and you to me,
Have no fear you see because I am not who I appear to be...

Lillie Lane

Chapter Fifteen

Many of my ancestors didn't have anything beyond an eighth-grade education, yet they managed to cultivate their necessities out of the resources bestowed upon us by nature. My grandmother would speak of senescent cells and how to flush them using lilac, goat's weed, and others in a blend. She knew how to nurture the fruits and wines of the land to produce longevity. When she began her bout with lymphedema, I would boil poke tea to ease her symptoms. I learned how not to activate the poisons but rather harvest the healing properties of the pokeweed plant. Mother Earth is kind to those who seek knowledge as a cure for the world's ills, rather than a cancer to its most precious gifts.

I studied briefly with the Khoisan people of Southern Africa, undertaking endeavors in ethnobotany as they taught me of their ancient herbal medicinal practices. Their remedies were thorough and time-tested, consisting of treatments for all sorts of issues including managing blood sugar and cholesterol levels, breaking fevers, and ridding the body of inflammation and urinary tract infections. We compared notes on various other plant concoctions to aid in the treatment of physiological and spiritual conditions.

In my travels throughout Ghana and Nigeria, I met a Chinese-American woman. Her name was Zhiong, and she introduced herself to me as Bear. She was studying, like me, but a subject far more serious by American educational standards; International Business. As we came to know each other, Bear told me of her migration to the United States from Chongqing, and of her love for the authentic foods of her familial home. She relished the spoils of nature, like me, and made music with her language as she spoke, culling the most passionate senses from within my mix. When my travels led me elsewhere, I longed for her conversation. Her friendship, platonic and pure, was an indefatigable desire to return to my own homelands, if only for a taste of my grandmother's cooking.

Grandma's kitchen epitomized the stillness of a world without artifice, without politics. It was comforting and numbing, falling victim to the mindset of the marginalized that underestimates our power to dismantle systems. My grandmother's stories were elixir, her words flowing like potions as she spoke and gave me words of wisdom to guide my life. Her anecdotes were the examples that cautioned my unbridled passions and emboldened my wildest dreams. I remembered my grandmother's accounts of the segregated South and of her own participation in the sit-ins referenced in history books, or her walks to school as a child being tormented by white students and school bus drivers passing by.

With a barely audible comment in her native tongue, Bear affirmed my perspective on the dualities of life in a world where opposing ideals must coexist in harmony but rarely, if ever, do. Hearing her speak with the Sichuanese dialect of the ethnic minority she'd been birthed into was satisfying in its subtle challenge of the heavy-handed nature of globalization and social conformity. Our language allowed us a sense of autonomy over our lives and a preservation of our sacred secrets and traditions.

Growing up, the folks over in Bluffton and Beaufort would call our Gullah verracular "plantation Creole." White folks always place labels on things they don't understand, regarding our speech as an impediment denoting ignorance or low social status. But the buckruh weren't Binyah, weren't our folks, so their words didn't make us no never mind.

I remember whenever my nana would have something to tell all of us, she'd send word by the oldest grandchild and expect it to get to each of us.

"Cumbaya, and bring the chillum, lemme talk to ya. Don't you carry bone either now, ya hear?" My oldest cousin was a gossip queen and the whole town knew about her big mouth. When we arrived, nana would have a big bowl of yams ready in the kitchen. "Dey yah, right here by my feet. Listen close."

She'd start off asking about our day, then tell us one of her fascinating stories based in Gullah folklore, then eventually build up to the surprise. After we left, she'd tell my aunt off about her oldest daughter whose figure was starting to draw the eyes of older men in the village. "Guh de ooman boonkey gettin' so big, she growing and spreading every which a way innit?"

Bear understood the sentimentality of these reflections and related them to her own conversations with her father at her nai nai's circular coffee table. They talked about the old ways of China, of preferential treatment and radical nationalism, and found similarities in the disparate impact of power structures that didn't reserve a place for them in traditional political systems.

I traveled far and wide across the continent in search of clear understanding. Along the way, I was reinvigorated by my encounter with the Nupe people of Nigeria, from who my fraternity derived the inspiration for our alias as Nupes. This tribe was an important minority in Kwara State and Kogi State. Their tribal marks were drawn on with many curves on the cheeks or one vertical stripe on each cheek. The scars are sometimes to highlight prestige or to identify the family of which a Nupe belongs.

Another group, the Hadza tribe of northern Tanzania, gave me a glimpse into the world of true hunter-gatherers.

They identified natural plant uses and tracked down prey using the clicks that dominated their language of Hadzane. I engaged with them in Swahili, recanting stories about our Damu lineage. They spoke of a world without the Western concepts of age or time and how the lack of traditional social stratification helps them maintain a truly egalitarian way of life.

I knew that I would one day return to a world that knows no balance, where capitalism controlled the culture and tendered fissures amongst populations of people devoid of hope. I summoned Olokun, praying for prosperity and peace for my troubles so that I might one day have enough to give freely back to those aspiring to greatness in their own right…the ones who dared to dream.

The more I called upon my ancestors, however, the more I became haunted by horrific images of total devastation. It was weird. As a kid, I used to stay up late at night so I wouldn't have nightmares of the Boo Hag. It was an evil spirit that rode your chest or back at night and tried its best to kill you in your sleep. It came in different forms, mine most often in the form of an old woman or marsh monster, and it would leave my body feeling drained each time I awoke.

For the first time since I was a boy, a Boo Hag visited me one night. I didn't have the hairbrush or colander or any of the other traditional protectors by my bed stand like I once did, and I was tormented by the symbolism of the visit when I awoke. Something dangerous was lurking in the shadows of my life, something evil even.

One evening after dinner, as I stumbled along the dimly lit path still tasting the sorghum beer from supper, an old blind woman appeared to me. I thought it odd, but I maintained a level of courtesy and respect for the elder when she spoke to me. Her accent was heavy, but she spoke English. "You hear that thunda?"

"No ma'am," I replied.

"Well, honey, you better put your listening ears on because there's a storm a-comin.'"

"You think so?" I asked out of genuine curiosity, wondering how she could be so sure.

"Yeah, there's something devilish brewing just over yonder, past them hills."

She vanished as quickly as she came, leaving me even more confused about what I'd just witnessed or whether I had. I heard her voice lingering in my head, mumbling something about fate and fire. Not having the slightest idea what she meant, I shook it off as old woman banter, or intoxication even. The sky was clear and life in this moment was as fine as it could possibly be if I ignored the minor inconveniences, half-regrets, and uncertainty of my future. Perhaps had I been more purposeful in my listening I would have realized the figurative nature of her warning and foreseen the carnage coming next.

There was something ominous in the atmosphere. As would be expounded on more eloquently in coming years, too many Americans espoused equality in theory, but not in application. There was an increasing swath of the population for whom the American dream was in rapid decline. While it still held true in theory, the unfortunate truth was that for marginalized groups, no matter how hard they tried, they would almost never make it. The powers that be would love us in public but hate us behind closed doors, where decisions were made about our livelihood. This bigoted ignorance, inherited through past generations, is the incessant echo of replacement theory and white superiority that haunts our nation. The fear that accompanied that haunting history was even more detrimental.

Politics, for that reason, was often viewed through our lens as the wrong kind of place for the right kind of people.

While I wandered the lands of my forefathers searching for people to heal, the United States was on the brink of being a nation in shambles. The whole world watched in helpless amazement as the president desecrated the civility and integrity of the greatest office on Earth. Then we cocked our heads in utter confusion and disbelief as prominent congressmen sent their careers up in smoke behind his destructive tactics. The house built on blood-soaked freedom had been all but set ablaze and burned to the ground, along with the morality of America.

We were approaching a critical election, and the entire year leading up to the ordeal had been fraught with politically charged attacks. As expected, when the election results came in late on the night of November 8th, there was significant unrest. On all sides of the political spectrum, there was displeasure with what was believed to be a sham of an election. Full certification of the results didn't come until nearly two months after ballots were cast, once there'd been ample opportunity for double and triple recounts. No one party truly won. What became known as the new "shot heard round the world," an up-close assassination attempt at the new president-elect, would mark the death knell to America's democracy.

In my mind, I returned to my last days in America. I'd packed my bags and headed further down south on a bus to begin this new life. Once there, I'd board a ship bound for my new home across the Atlantic. The recent rampage of domestic terrorism persuaded me against flying. I remember arriving at the Greyhound station in Atlanta, utterly bewildered by the events and faces before me. It was a chaotic nightmare of dysfunction. Crime was rampant in this particular area of downtown.

Outside, awaiting our arrival, armed security guards rushed us into the station as we unloaded the bus, cautioning us that robberies were frequent here and that it was safest for us to wait inside until our next departure. Inside, it smelled horribly of urine and feces throughout, and everyone working there seemed especially irritated with anyone who dared ask a question in an effort to decipher the confusion. There were no available seats in the waiting area; many homeless and unkempt individuals lined the walls and crowded the empty spaces on the floor. This left most people standing, tired and weighed down with baggage in anticipation of our respective destinations.

A woman who was completely overwhelmed with the task of motherhood let her little girl run freely about the building, wreaking havoc and expending as much energy as the kid could to wear herself out. The mother let strangers feed the girl candy and other snacks, anything to keep her daughter out of her hair for a temporary period of respite. The woman yelled at the little girl every so often at the top of her lungs, to no avail. Finally, the mother loaded the little girl up with melatonin, attempting to find peace. Once back on the bus, she grew furious as her daughter vomited everywhere in the seat, presumably because of the smorgasbord of junk she'd just eaten over the last hour or so. The woman cursed and yelled loudly, disturbing the sleeping passengers on this red eye bus ride as she struggled to cope with the realities of her incompetence as a parent. It was sad to see; so abysmal, in fact, that I thanked God again for not having had any children and asked Him to take His time in blessing me with any. I vowed to spend at least another three years of life developing and maximizing my own happiness before I became responsible for that of someone else's.

Most alarming about my observations there, however, was not that there are people who don't care about putting their ignorance and insufficiency on display for the world to see. I noticed the heavy presence of Army soldiers in and out of this place, which had recently become a de facto hub for transfers to various bases throughout the South. They were young, baby-faced, and hard not to study in their fatigues. The looks of gloom on these soldiers' faces were a telling sign of the doom to come. At the time, I assumed their looks of terror, indifference, and disgust were indictments of these new—albeit temporary—surroundings as they waited to be shipped to the next hell hole. Or maybe they dreaded their decision to enlist in the first place. When I think back, maybe they knew something the rest of us didn't about what might play out over the next few years.

When I was young, straight out of middle school, I got my first pistol. This was years after my first shotgun. The pistol was dirty, of course, but it was cheap. A throw-away, really. Early on in life, I knew it would serve me well to know how to protect myself, using my hands, my mind, and my tools effectively as weapons. That first day my cousin laid that chrome piece with the pretty pearl handle in my hands, he told me to always keep one thing in mind with this metal of mass destruction: "Don't tote it if you don't know what to do with it or if you ain't gonna use it when it's time to."

Ever since then, I've been on go anytime it's on me. What he didn't mention though, was the second lesson after that. Quickly I learned that there is a certain discernment that you must develop to understand when it's truly time to act and when you should fall back, fight another time, or in another way. Some situations just throw all the rules of engagement out of the window, however.

My political acumen was relatively high in comparison to most; I'd worked on Capitol Hill for a while between degrees and seen a lot of the savagery in politics that most weren't privy to. There were times I'd lure certain affinity groups into political discussions espousing the very views I worked tirelessly in opposition of, to gauge my peers' perspectives and brainstorm means of achieving the mission we collectively sought. Spirited debate would often turn into emotional displays when frail minds failed to realize the intent of objective dialogue in close circles. I appreciated the ability to engage in sparring sessions as an opportunity to get to know my counterparts while sharpening my sword for the inevitable civil war brewing.

While overseas, I'd reconnected with an old college friend named Elara who I ran into on a safari expedition in Kenya. We were both there for a few days and decided to go explore local scenes to wind down after the previous days' events. We'd talked and laughed and ate and danced and before you know it, we kissed. It was magical and left us wanting more of each other. When she returned to her job at the U.S. Embassy in Cairo, Egypt, I called her often and chatted with her about my journey across the continent thus far. We spoke of Cape Town, Madagascar, Malawi, Liberia, Tanzania, and all the other places we'd either visited or wanted to. We talked of children and what we might name our little girl, who would be a spitting image of her mother and possess the grace of a Queen with the sharp intellect of a doctor or lawyer. We dreamt of days spent together on beaches, having picnics, and running wild with laughter as we engaged in the silliest games. But life as it were, in the trenches, did not lend itself well to child-bearing. We were career-focused and still seeking financial security in our respective lives. Poverty is a crippling condition, and time a fleeting one. We neither had money nor time, and thought it cruel to attempt to raise a child in that environment. We knew that this energy between us was too great to set aside, however, and vowed to become official whenever I returned to the Motherland.

Now that I had found love again and started thinking of what family life would be like, I was even more on edge about the uncertainties of tomorrow. I was taking heads off expeditiously behind my family, my Blood. I didn't want to lose them nor for them to lose me, but if it ever became a necessity, I would lay it all on the line. It's a blessing to have the gifts of freedom and life, but I've also always prepared for war and what comes along with it. I have to be.

...And so it began.

Life's Library

Someone asked me the other day to describe myself in
    one word, how absurd?
I am life's library, a living account of all things good and
    bad,
Turn to a page that makes you rejoice with laughter,
Turn to another that makes you cringe in pain,
I am all of the above,
Life's living library—peace, happiness, and love,
Ask me who I am today,
Tomorrow my answer won't be the same,
I am but a variable player in life's constant game,
No one chapter of mine is the same—constantly
    seeking betterment of self,
My past is history, piled up on a shelf,
Peer reviews are misconstrued without peering
    within—be not fooled by external disguise...open
    me like your favorite novel and penetrate me with
    your eyes,
Indulge me with your intellect and your inquisition,
    soak me with your tears,
And through the years—
You shall come to understand me,
Like the man who has read the worn pages of his most
    beloved book over and over again,
He is no longer reading for pleasure...his pupils, tired
    and weary,
His face, wrinkled and eerie;
Back bent and brow furrowed as he carries a load that
    no one man alone can bear,

A collection of thoughts, emotions, experiences...he is
    me, we are the dreams of our ancestry,
So when asked once again who I am, I reply,
I am a "Gringot," I rejoice, I cry,
I am a complex individual full of knowledge—I am war,
    I am tranquility, I am hate, I am love,
I am life's library; I am all of the above.

         Lillie Lane

Chapter Sixteen

I emerged from the bathroom, buttoning my shirt as she lay back down to rest from the long night we shared before my departure. Watching the muted television as foreign images of chaos flashed across the screen while international news anchors commented of America's demise was a nightmare neither of us were quite ready for. Here, Elara was safe from the melee. I peeked over at her through the mirror, saw her fall asleep as Nina Simone's "I Put a Spell on You" faded out in the background.

Her body was still. I stood there for a seconds taking in the quaintness of the quietude. Sometimes sleep is the supreme solace. The night before, we'd fallen asleep holding each other through sobs of serendipity, grateful for the chance encounter that had brought us together. I tried to tell her that I understood if life was no good without a partner, and that I wouldn't mind if somehow my body was left behind on the battlefield. She needn't worry her spirit about moving on; someone else could make this a home in my absence, but her soul would be mine until the end of this lifetime and into the next. There was no way to frame it delicately; I took precaution to speak the possibility of no return without falter in reassurance that we would soon reconnect. Yet, I couldn't shake the feeling that whatever would transpire in the days, months, and years to come would rock our commitment to its core, and that it was quite feasible the ashes would find me in their midst when the dust had settled, and we would be no more.

"After all we've been through together, you decide to take the easy way out instead of just telling me you no longer want me? Tell me, is there someone else?" she asked incredulously. I let out a ight-hearted laugh, twisting my face in confusion. How or why she jumped to the conclusion of infidelity in that moment is beyond me. I told her the truth, that I had been running my whole life – from failure, from fear, from frustrated purposes far too great in number to revisit…and it pained me that I may never outrun my former self to find a love I felt worthy of. She listened patiently as I poured my heart out in pity of myself. Then she laughed gently before shaking her head and clearing her throat. She held my face in her hands, looking through the tears starting to flood my eyes and peered at the little boy that lay behind them, broken and confused. She told me something she'd heard her grandmother say to her brother countless times: "Baby, a man without a past is a man without a story, and a man without a story is a man without substance. It is the journey that creates the juice; how can you truly appreciate the sweet taste of life if you've never known its bitterness before the ripening?" Then she gave me a squeeze, and I smiled sweetly at her in agreement. "Elara, this love we have is everlasting, and I'll always be here as long as you let me," I responded. "May God's mercy get me home, and God's grace get us through." After all, we needed each other.

I tucked her spell book back into the drawer, beneath the stack of papers that concealed its presence. I put on my boots as I shed a tear, reminiscing on the halcyon days of a period long past, a reflection of the type of peace that would never again present itself upon my doorstep. Oh, how I longed for those times when things were much simpler, when life's bitter lemons seemed just a tad bit sweeter. But alas, this is war.

And so we fought. Hard. Heavy in number. Huge in spirit. We were tactical and equipped in every capacity. There were different factions with slightly varied functions and we operated in accord with one another. That's the way it was always supposed to be.

President Drumpfelt, now out of office but emboldened by a radicalized base on a warpath for revenge, leveraged the current climate for unprecedented carnage against the American people and political system. As racial tension increased, so did the erosion of critical social systems. Drumpfelt used demagogic lexicon to manipulate minds into defying logic for the sake of self-righteousness. Simultaneously, I witnessed my scared profession being transformed before my eyes as I sat helpless and terrified.

One alarming offshoot of this brewing war was the deregulation of artificial intelligence and its effects on marginalized communities. Despite the advent of technology, AI was, in effect, accelerating us into the past and all of its bigoted glory. Prejudice was inherent in all of our societal systems, but medicine was now being manipulated by a force perceivably stronger than man. Bias baked into AI would give rise to a wave of robotic racism, granting shelter to medical institutions who would extend the blame for missed diagnoses and mass deaths beyond human oversight or the lack thereof.

Who would hold the machines accountable if men can't even account for their own errors? It didn't help that across the nation, hospital operations were increasingly being acquired by private equity groups with ill intentions. These groups were capable of operating under veils of secrecy with minimal regulatory oversight, with information about the investors and other key asset information locked tight within a black box. Dark money filled these voids and scaled the attacks on quality of care. History was rife with this manner of brilliant bigotry. As if the past wasn't enough, it was once more becoming open season on Black bodies, on women, on the desperate and voiceless.

A group of "melanated MDs" had formed a secret coalition of physicians on call for the cause, ready to provide their services in support of comrades across the Atlantic. A friend of mine from school connected me and I quickly got to work using analytics to target regions termed "medically deficient," a diagnosis categorized by eighteen factors that included areas with too few primary care providers, high infant mortality or poverty rates, high elderly populations, and significant cultural or geographical barriers. We followed the trail of private equity healthcare acquisitions like sharks behind ships during the Middle Passage. Together, we modeled a sort of Underground Railroad for medicine and supporting comrades in the trenches.

Sometime after my arrival, I was summoned by my mother as she lay sick on a hospital bed suffering from a number of complications. She didn't know at the time, but she'd been poisoned by one of her colleagues in the liberation movement and, in the process, had contracted a deadly virus. I spoke to her through muffled tears as she attempted to make out what was on her mind through painful, paradoxical breaths. She urged me to travel to her place and look under the floorboards beneath the old wood chest of drawers in the corner of her bedroom. There I would find the answer I was looking for in my quest for (medical) freedom for my people.

When I arrived, what I found blew me away. The handwriting was all too familiar. I uncovered stacks of stained parchment paper to find mom's notes with the patents for industry-altering medical techniques. These were ideas initiated by my great grandfather, the root doctor, from whom I'd drawn much of my inspiration. My mother and father had worked secretly on perfecting these blueprints in collaboration for years, before my father gave up on the idea. Somehow, using their engineering and programming acuity, they were able to isolate contaminated cells to use a crystal-enhanced laser procedure to directly target problem areas and solve elusive problems (like cancer, which would have been groundbreaking research). After a bitter split between the two of them, my father cursed the plans and detached his name from any further developments with this experiment. His new medical vision didn't align with the wasted efforts of a dream that may never come true in his eyes.

By then, my mother was even more motivated to counter the evils of the exploitative healthcare industry and she'd spoken out frequently and feverishly against its predatory practices. Little did I know how much of a target that would place on her head while I was away. Mama had garnered national attention in her movement to liberate marginalized Americans from the manipulative monopolies of Westernized medical treatment. One of her biggest obstacles was the steady rise of inflation coupled with dark money in politics and its unforeseen impact on organizing. It now cost a lot more to do this work and secure campaigns against malicious actors or dilutive agendas. As such, it became harder and harder to reach the minds of those who most needed her help, and the grassroots coalition had struggled to build the necessary support.

I found a half-finished note addressed to Dr. Kizzy Korbett, possibly one my mother had put down just moments before her house was raided by agents looking for evidence of anything that could put her away. "May you never want again. Take care. Fight hard." Those would be the words offered to my mom's comrades as she consoled them in their efforts to overturn the healthcare system in America. If only I'd known, maybe I could have protected her.

Black venture capitalists saved the planet. The rise of cyber warfare against targeted demographic groups compelled a different means of defense. When the government defunded and threatened hospitals that wouldn't acquiesce to their ideology and control, those VCs stepped up to infuse crowd-funding capital into relief operations. They leveraged their networks to pour money into a special purpose acquisition company (SPAC) that secretly operated the entire underground operations of the Healing Road. There was Octavia Torres, Lo Robinson, Drew, Zo, Toussaint, and Russ at the helm. Adorn was the chief conductor and she was a modern-day Harriet in her own right. The way she collaborated with Mother Mack, who was often regarded as an eerie reincarnation of Marie Laveau, offered a dynamic duo of Black power aligned in the fight for equity and elevation of the most historically marginalized population on the planet.

Black women were dying at an alarming rate and Western science did not care. With the widening rift in political philosophies and the reversal of key civil rights legislation, segregation had resurfaced on American shores and the quality of care available for impoverished, minority communities suffered consequently. For that reason, I was willing to live and die on my own terms. Reverse engineered mining outfits leveraged energy reduction to shift crypto assets funding the war into the hands of grassroots Black ops groups focused on counter surveillance. The entire plan was genius.

Eventually, we employed Black doctors in every major hospital in America, myself included. There was a need for oversight of white physicians and prejudicial practices in hospitals where so many Black bodies were entering and not returning, especially during the height of the Coronavirus pandemic. Children and the elderly were suffering. Schools were closed. Fresh food was in scarce supply. Families were being torn apart by mandatory quarantine protocols. This mysterious virus had crept out of nowhere and was now mutating by the minute it seemed, with new strains popping up one after the other wreaking havoc on our healthcare systems. While most Coronavirus patients did not succumb to its deathly destruction, its most devastating effects were being felt in communities where resources were limited and the healthcare was mediocre if not wholly inadequate, and Black Americans were increasingly being diagnosed with the virus before dying days later.

I signed up for the task of overseeing medical operations. I was employed by San Columbus Valley Regional Hospital, one of the top locations in the Midwest for major surgeries. The chief physician was a snarling, sexist Southerner who'd been uprooted from the gulf coast of Alabama and placed in a role with a disturbing amount of discretionary control over the affairs of patients who entered his domain. There were talks of plague-inducing biochemical warfare supplied by the government that was to be employed against the economically downtrodden and undesirables. Of course, anyone with a brain knew what this was code for. It was a form of population control, with the Coronavirus concentrated in areas where the healthcare was egregiously inadequate.

Despite the current climate, Black doctors were thriving like never before. Mysteriously, the virus numbers in our community were suddenly lower than anywhere else in the world. No one could figure out the answer to our "magic," as they called it, but it was nothing but that good medicine... the kind they can't sell you at the store. I prayed to Olokun for healing before addressing the wounds and impurities of others, and that made all the difference. They called me "The Healer," because I showed those fancy T10 doctors what to do with nothing but herbs from the Earth. We saved over 70,000 lives.

Sometimes I would fly South for the weekend, to observe the disparities by region. I was always repulsed at the smell of death, which was now so frequent that funeral homes could no longer keep up with the supply of fresh corpses on a daily basis. Many people were buried in shallow dirt holes in pine boxes, a reversion to burial tactics of the 1940s. It was funny in a way how, in the South particularly, you could always tell the demographics of a church based on its cemetery. The dead had a way of speaking from the grave and allowing you to feel their anger, their pain, their resentment.

When I look back over the years I gave fighting for myself and others, I didn't regret them. I couldn't. Like my childhood days eating cherries from the tree and watching the harvest suddenly grow dry with the changing climate, these memories were a part of me. These experiences helped make me who I am. Some people said I was an asshole. Some say I was too relentless in my efforts to impose change. Maybe I wore my heart on my sleeve and was slow to trust because of my observations. Maybe I was too harsh in demanding my respect. Something in my soul just wouldn't let me rest with the evils of the world brewing against my people. I had been blessed with gifted hands to do the work of my ancestors, freeing anyone who would heed the whistle-call of salvation. Long gone were the days of bowing to a system that did not accommodate or even give consideration to our needs. Only now, I vowed to wage peace and not war against my fellow man.

I was asked by a young woman once on my way to engage stakeholders about ways to secure more contributions for our cause, "Do you match your dollars with deeds, Mr. Cole?" How insightful. It was the Robin Hood reasoning all over again.

Sure, raising money for a worthy objective was admirable, but was it enough?

The next week I went back to work, still thinking about what she'd implied. I knew that I could do more in this fight. And when the racist Governor of South Carolina, Bob Hunt, was admitted to my hospital I knew that my moment of sacrifice had come. For all of the sanctioned killing of Black bodies he allowed under his watch, for all of the policies he directed diminishing Black patient care and eliminating safe alternatives for their healthcare needs, I owed this to my people. Though I didn't believe in playing God, I truly believed his arrival here was no coincidence. It was time to do what so many of my white colleagues had done to women who look like my mother, my grandmother, my future wife…

So I sent Hunt to hell to meet his maker. And I relished in the simplistic beauty of the decision, felt free having let go of the socialized concepts of civility and met fire with brimstone. As I pulled the plugs from his state-of-the-art, life-saving medical devices, I felt a wave of justice come over me. It was my way of speaking for the silenced, for the women everywhere who'd been tormented by his discriminatory tactics and harmed by his hateful ways. And you know what I found out? Giving voice to our values is one of the most liberating things in the world.

The moment was spoiled by someone I thought was a fellow comrade. There were two Black doctors in this entire hospital. The only other one besides myself was Dr. Aaron Anderson, the grandson of the great Dr. Benjamel Anderson, a luminary of neurology and pathology. Aaron and I kept our distance from each other, tending to our own hefty patient schedule and varying array of responsibilities. I knew he was a little "different" than the rest of us in this fight, but what I didn't know was that he wasn't in this fight with us at all. In fact, he was a spy working for the government to upend any insurgencies. He was hiding in plain sight, plotting against us right under our own noses. While it was fine to be amongst the opposition, Aaron was Black scum, a stain on the long list of accomplishments by his grandfather and our ancestors. Despite his medical brilliance he was devoid of self-value. Further, he was imbibed with the self-loathing elixir that flowed to Black healthcare professionals appointed to serve in one of our nation's preeminent de facto preferential systems. Notwithstanding the relegate conditions of minority physicians' career prospects, adversity never absolves one of moral bankruptcy. Aaron was another Uncle Ruckus, no relation whatsoever. It was his testimony against me that sent me to my fate in the South Carolina State Penitentiary.

Lady Justice

With a slip of her cloak she revealed herself to me ever
so slightly,
Appeasing my curiosity with her generosity,
Indulging my foolish desires of grandeur,
Slapping me back to reality ever so often;
Her philosophy accosted me, so compelling in its
imposition that I couldn't stifle the demands of the
call,
My ears perked at the sound of her cry,
The beautiful, deceitful motions of her dances offered
little more than starched papers and palpitations as
receipt of her favor,
Her touch lacerating in its disguise as love,
Oh, to be stricken with such passion...
Envious and burdened by a system that creates more
victims than victors,
The meek succumb to the retracted scales of justice,
leaving us helpless in a world where it is seemingly
just...us.

Chapter Seventeen

The trial was the longest I'd ever held my breath before. It felt like I'd drowned by the time the verdict was delivered. Voir dire was a sham. An aged, all-white panel acted as my peers for 3 whole days while they judged me with contemptuous indifference. They saw my outer shell and, failing to engage on a connective level, recognized an opportunity to strip me of my humanity even further.

I remembered the village mothers, whose pulchritudinous personas embodied all that was pure and true and wholesome. Their energy channeled spirits of goodwill and nurturing without regard for their own limitations and unmet needs. The joy their hugs brought to the faces of little Black boys like me dared us to dream of a life we all longed for, but few would attain. Their faces were a depiction of undying hope, which resonated with me in this moment. I was more than my past. I began to dip deeper through the Rolodex of memories, curating those bits and pieces – the smiles, the laughs, the good times – to carry with me forward into tomorrow. I prepared for life after temporary death, knowing fully that beyond these walls, the status quo of social stigma would bind itself to me for as long as I let it. I would need to be intentional – not about hiding the scars but redefining their meaning and conveying the lessons learned from each of them.

It had only been seventeen weeks, yet I was so far from being acclimated to this new environment that I doubted I ever would be. Alone in my cell, I looked to the Heavens for help. Though we'd never spoken directly, my belief had been affirmed a thousand times over that God was up there somewhere, east of the sun, west of the moon. People often became dazed and confused at my talks of spirituality, especially my references to the identity of the Divine being. To me, God isn't gender conforming. I think God shows up in the way most relatable to you.

Though I've used He and She interchangeably over the years, I personally believe that God is a Black woman. Black women surrounded me with love from the time I was charged with felony murder for the death of Governor Hunt to the time I was sentenced. They celebrated when I walked out of the courtroom smiling, fully embracing my newfound martyr status. Unlike my brothers, who offered little more than words of comfort throughout my trial, Black women wrote me letters and sent me money for commissary, making sure I'd never be in need during my time here. When I think of unconditional love even when I'm undeserving of it, or tireless labor on behalf of the masses often without credit, or forgiveness and nurturing of the world's burdens beyond no other, Black women stand out as the staple. Their essence gives everlasting life, their will forges ways out of none.

As chow time approached, my mind drifted back to memories of meals past and how my grandmother would find solace in her kitchen. The culinary creations she crafted from deep-welled pots and cast-iron pans were iterations of unconditional love. I felt God in her food. We'd always lived off the fat of the land, and the essence of nature that derived from it had always fed my spirit in ways beyond the superficial feelings of pleasure that we often find throughout life. The smells emanating from grandma's house on any given day touched the depths of my soul, and it was from there that they arose in this moment, wafting through the prison walls and filling my nostrils with nostalgic bliss. I imagined this was what death row felt like, awaiting that final meal that would take you back to a positive place, unlike this pit of persecution.

I sat down to write. It had been awhile. Things were noticeably different this time. I felt the emotions flow deep, trickling down like tears and converting the energy into my pen. When I wrote, the words stained the page. There was pain in this poem. Somber in this song. Tragedy in this testimony. And yet, it was a tribute to the true test of a man. May I pass with flying colors or die trying before I ever cower in the face of defeat. That's definite. What may seem uncertain to the world is that this iteration was summoned out of love...the kind my mother showed me, and the kind my father didn't. Both were equally effective in giving me a broad ranging outlook on life and what it means to live. I need the masses to know that love is a language of its own that must be studied and refined, but can never be mastered to perfection.

One of the true tests of a man denotes an underlying reverence for the concept of love, in all its glory and gore. I didn't have it all—rarely had anything, frankly—but I consistently gave what I had. That revelation, for me, was the culmination of a lifetime of sorrows that became successes when I changed my perspective. Victory was sweet, but defeat was necessary to refine my taste for certain aspects of it and I savored those moments, knowing that I was equipped with everything I needed to handle anything I might face.

As money and ambition go, the difference between hunger and greed is an illumination of your own palatable philosophy. The line between need and greed is undoubtedly thin, however concerned with the balance one may be. Many I know chose to live life on the edge. For better or worse, there is no rectification for reward or remorse.

All of my tomorrows are based on a nation that sees the errors of its ways and gets better, but I must live with my existence in a world that doesn't, and likely never will. However brief my time left may be here, I must carry myself as if there is always a brighter day awaiting if I continue striving.

Perhaps one of the most agonizing aspects of my anticipated release was the financial consideration. I needed a way to get back on my feet, a way to redeem myself. I needed money for sustenance; plus, it was one of those unfortunate truths that once you fall victim to the system, it owns you forever. No job. No public housing options. No second chance or acknowledgment of rehabilitation, as society often likes to suggest. That stigma often feels like a permanent stain, hideous and shameful under the piercing eyes of the world, even if limited to our own conscience.

I thought about my mother and how her anointing had always covered me despite my transgressions. I remembered her calm in the roughest of storms, her ability to manage trials and turmoil much greater than my own. I never saw her skip a beat, even when her back was against the wall and there was no way out in sight. Gospel was her escape. Suddenly, memories of her swaying to *Sounds of Blackness* with her eyes closed brought me back. The music filled my ears and as I heard her crooning softly it took me to a place of peace. I finally understood. Her unwavering faith kept her going, and it was that same faith that brought me out of the darkness that clouded my mind in this cell.

When I reflected on my life, I did so with the belief and contentment that I gave what I had. That gave me peace. I had fought valiantly against two of my greatest enemies. There was the beast of burden and then there was the beast of blame; both were masters that manipulated the mind into a crippling state of despair. Pain is often a necessary inconvenience of life; if you embrace and channel it accordingly, you can become stronger than you ever imagined.

Time

Beyond the beaten path,
Where the red ferns grow and the trees bring darkness
    with their shade,
Where the wind whispers through the leaves into our
    soul almost as if to say:
"Rest now ye troubles my child,
Sit still for a while,
Embrace the magic within and around you,
Become one with the energies and powers that be,
You are they and they are you—
Yet you're different all the same,"
This is the place where heavy hearts come to lie,
Where worries are no more and the limit becomes the
    sky,
Never-ending and abundant in its blessings,
The Earth gives in bountiful beauty unbeknownst to
    those who blind themselves with the superficial,
The supernatural creates what is actual if only we open
    our eyes and believe,
"Breathe...be at ease once again with the sorrows of
    life, for they are but a faction of the dream—a small
    price we pay to be great,
As Mother Nature gives, she must also take,
Leaving in her wake a mass of pleasure and pain,
    development and destruction, sunshine and rain..."
And where death does its due, life becomes anew,
Creating opportunities for me and for you if only we
    remain true
To the gifts that lay within us,

Lillie Lane

Bestowed upon us with the utmost care and
    responsibility that we shall one day share with the
    world,
There is no greater love under the sky,
Than to be chosen by the Divine,
A tale as old as time,
A tale as old as time...

Chapter Eighteen

They say the difference between men and boys are the lessons they learn. My father, through his absences and transgressions, taught me plenty—but he was wealthy and well-liked, which made him relatively immune to the scrutiny given other fleeting fathers, despite his pigmented skin. It wasn't that he was completely absent, it was that he wasn't there when it mattered. In the past, we'd gone extended periods without talking—months that became years. It was almost as if we became strangers through his success.

We missed out on each other's major accomplishments—my all-conference honors and white coat ceremony, his rise to Surgeon General and Forbes' power lists. My father was hard on me, and in many ways I appreciated it, but there were some parts of him that were hard to love. His teaching method had always consisted of demands, rather than demonstrations. We had an estranged relationship that developed as I eventually became of drinking age. Coincidentally, his love of whisky would eventually get the best of him as he continuously drowned his emotions in bourbon. It was maybe the only time we could see eye to eye, with a glass in our hands. Unfortunately, he passed away soon after my departure to Africa, and I never got to thank him for those moments together.

So often in life, we reflect on the negatives. We remember what people didn't give or haven't done instead of all the things they did. We constantly focus on what's missing instead of all of the gifts in our possession. Maneuvering through life while maintaining such a disposition, viewing our circumstances through a lens of lack instead of plentitude, will almost always equate to a miserable, insufferable existence marked by incessant dissatisfaction.

For most of us, life is a long, winding road full of pain, promise (mostly unfulfilled), and, if you're lucky enough, purpose. Without a doubt, one of the most challenging parts of this journey is acknowledging the ways in which the pain of our past hinders our promise, and instead of allowing that hurt to fester, healing ourselves by turning our pain into purpose.

One morning, I woke up to the news that my conviction had been vacated. I was finally free. There was no explanation, only a note left with my belongs when I went to collect them. "For those of us who remain nurtured by nostalgia, instead of seeking comfort in the challenge and uncertainty of changed circumstances. Never forget." The cryptic nature of the words was unsettling, but my mind was too consumed with my return to the real world to focus on anything but freedom.

The flaws in our legal system that create skewed applications of justice are fatal in many ways to the individuals affected by them. Instead of facilitating the true spirit of the law, we end up creating more victims, hampering our economic productivity, weakening our democracy, and casting hope aside for so many who regard it as all they have left in this life.

It was only through the grant of grace that I was able to walk the path of enlightenment and find true understanding. The more of it I gave to others, the more I was able to resonate with their actions in a way that removed the ego and empathized with them wherever they were on their life's journey. This awakening helped me see life with a clearer eye and erase the hate from my heart. I'd spent decades engulfed in enmity for people and things which I had no real understanding of. Perhaps, that is the saddest truth about running out of time with the people, places and things you hold dear.

Suffice it to say, I'm grateful for my father. The assignments I'd been given as I traveled through adulthood were successful in large part because of the lessons he'd taught me over the years. Though I often talk of his contributions to my life from a perspective of lack, he truly gave me what I needed to be a better man and to be self-sufficient in those times that simply being a man wasn't enough. His toughness got me through, and my mother's blessings got me over. Glory!

The day came for me to make the long trip home. Times had changed for sure. We had a newly elected democratic government, and a president who sympathized with my situation. After months of political posturing, the president had agreed on terms to vacate my remaining sentence. I had received a pardon. In exchange for my release, I accepted a commitment to teaching the gospel of my medicinal practices. I was given full control over the Bowman Institute of Medicine, a new minority-serving medical school established with the intention of increasing the ranks of Black and brown healthcare professionals. One of my first orders of business would be to compile the notes of my travels and of my great-grandfather into a book offering various case studies on holistic medicine and infectious diseases.

If there was anything my parents both believed in wholeheartedly, it was the idea of not resting on your laurels. "Yesterday is history; today is the start of your story. If you want to be great, make sure you act in a way that people can judge you accordingly." Though I'd lived a life worthy of celebration, everything I'd done to date was now in the past, and it was time to keep moving forward with the next opportunity. I approached this Bowman endeavor with the same hunger that I had with every other new and exciting experience years prior, knowing that I would need to prove myself all over again despite my

Lillie Lane

history of principled leadership in the medical profession. When the ribbons were cut and my office was unveiled, replete with the statue of Dr. Sebi (after whom the institute was named), I threw my head back and my hands up and rejoiced. After everything was all said and done, I could only hope that I'd made my ancestors proud and that they were looking down in adoration at what their hands and labor and love has produced.

Later that week, I returned to the island, to the one place I could call home, for the first time since I'd left to go overseas years ago. I pulled onto the dirt road and took in the familiar surroundings of my childhood. I saw the sign on the faded picket fence that marked the entrance to the family farm. I cringed at the ghastly sight of overgrown grass and broken farm equipment where the pasture used to be. There was no one there to greet me as there'd always been; everyone had grown old and gone away by now. Not only had the stock market crashed and wiped away most people's life savings during the war, the pandemic had also exacerbated the issues in rural communities and destroyed our economies to the point of extinction, forcing many people into suburban strongholds for a new chance at life. Mama had succumbed to the virus while I was away and transitioned peacefully, although entirely too soon. The emptiness of the place was eerily comforting to me.

I heard the wind whistle through the trees. I listened intently as the birds sang sweet songs of love and loss, of life and death, of spring beginnings and fall transitions. A voice came to me. An old scholar years past had challenged me to live a full life in service to humanity, whether through my words or actions or both. "Either write something worth reading or do something worth writing," he said. So I set out to do both.

Now, looking back over my life, I can confidently say that I've given all I have with nothing left to give. Patting myself on the back as dust swept around me and trees swayed once more in the breeze, I said quietly aloud, "Job well done."

I thought of my brother, who was set to be released one year from the day of my own, and I knew I'd be there to welcome him home. We would be reunited by the ambitions of law and medicine, and he would soon become an integral part of what I was building with the institute. I thought of my new students, and I knew that what we were about to accomplish together would surely transcend time. These scholars—each from communities where the odds were stacked high against them—were the reason for my existence. I couldn't have done it without the network of diverse professionals who, just like these students, had risen above unimaginable obstacles to be standing amongst giants in the present moment. They say the cream always rises to the top. Well, float on my brothers and sisters.

In that moment, something nudged me to a place behind the old barn where my brother and I used to play hide and seek. We would stash our secrets there, away from the eyesight of the elders. I looked under the big rock by the mulberry bush where we buried cans covered with pieces of tin and scraps. I felt an urge to dig deeper, as if something inside were calling out to me. Then I found it – a letter from my brother with newspaper clippings attached. There was no record of the Healing Road, nor of my heroic act against Governor Hunt. A headline highlighted his death "by natural causes." Another read "Tragic Passing of a True American Hero Sparks Truce Between Troops." A stalemate? That's the story they came up with for the end of the war?! My head was spinning with questions. How could this be? I almost missed the obituary clipped to the back of one of the articles. My face turned pale and I instantly became sick to my stomach.

They killed him. My brother, my best friend. They had silenced him after speaking out about the truths of the revolution. I felt a stabbing sensation as it set in. What hurt most is that I never got to protect him and redeem him the way he had for me. I had reached the pinnacle of my career and not been privy to its enjoyment, nor had I been present for the greatest moment of my life when my brother became a hero. He had been released some years prior – unknown to me – and found the cover-ups of the work I had done, the work our mother and father had initiated decades ago. I saw a half-finished letter denoting a new phenomenon called the "Mandela Effect." I wondered who he was writing to, if not me. Then I flipped the letter over and felt the stabbing sensation again. "I did it for mom, you would have been proud bro." His handwriting was chicken scratch, but I took pride in the beauty of those words and the clarity of purpose in his final moments.

I needed to find out more. I ran to the house, rummaging through his old room. I reached behind a worn cupboard where the walls concealed a false insert. From there, I withdrew what felt like a stack of newspapers. In them, folded neatly within the creases, were articles, one after another offering scholarly insights on a new plague of sorts. This mind-altering occurrence marked by false memories had taken hold of the population, leaving them convinced that certain events, as they knew them, had never happened. My contributions to the movement, the single event that had given significance to my life…all gone.

Mandela Effect. Had I been locked away that long? How would I even decipher what was real anymore? My chest suddenly grew tight with the realization that nothing but this image of home and the events of my life ingrained in my brain would the same as I once remembered. For all the world knows, they never happened. For me, they might as well be a distant memory.

Finally released from the agony of endless white walls, shocked by the changes of my childhood home—how much smaller it looked, the foreign smells that no longer brought delight to my nose…I dropped to my knees in the middle of the dirt path and wept. Some would say the good days are long gone, that we are living in the last days where traditional values, principles, and concepts of humanity are a distant memory. To the past, I offer these words as a toast honoring what is no more and celebrating what is to be.

I relished the moment as I sat there in the clay dirt, channeling the history of my past, remembering how I'd waited patiently in my cocoon for my butterfly moment. I'd finally found what I had been searching for, that nugget which had been left by my ancestors for me to go back and retrieve before pressing onward. The fight wasn't finished. In fact, it had just begun.

I inhaled a breath of fresh air, my lungs basked in its newness. I exhaled loudly, letting the old breath run its course. "Sankofa."